"Tell me why," Alexi insisted, the frustration disappearing to be replaced with something much more disturbing—genuine interest in me and my life, something I'd yearned for all through my teenage years.

"Tell me why you gave up on your dream," he repeated, his voice soft, coaxing. "And then I'll leave."

I opened my mouth, determined to give him an answer, any answer that would make him leave and take this pointless yearning away again. But the only explanation I could think of was the real one.

Because I have a child, a son, who I love more than life itself. And I'm the only person he has. I can't risk leaving him alone—dying the way Remy died. So I found a way to readjust my dreams. To feed my passion for racing—while also fulfilling my obligations to my child.

But I couldn't tell him that.

And then the door burst open and Cai ran into the room ten minutes early, a four-year-old bundle of energy...and the black hole in the pit of my stomach imploded. For the first time in my life I was not pleased to see him.

My time had run out.

Passion in Paradise

Exotic escapes...and red-hot romances!

Step into a jet-set world where first class is the *only* way to travel. From Monte Carlo to Tuscany, you'll find a billionaire at every turn! But no billionaire is complete without the perfect romance. Especially when that passion is found in the most incredible destinations...

Find out what happens in:

The Innocent's Forgotten Wedding by Lynne Graham

The Italian's Pregnant Cinderella by Caitlin Crews

Kidnapped for His Royal Heir by Maya Blake

His Greek Wedding Night Debt by Michelle Smart

The Spaniard's Surprise Love-Child by Kim Lawrence

My Shocking Monte Carlo Confession by Heidi Rice

A Bride Fit for a Prince? by Susan Stephens

A Scandal Made in London by Lucy King

Available this month!

Heidi Rice

MY SHOCKING MONTE CARLO CONFESSION

PRESENTS

Recycling programs
for this product may
not exist in your area.

ISBN-13: 978-1-335-14846-9

My Shocking Monte Carlo Confession

Copyright © 2020 by Heidi Rice

This edition published by arrangement with Harlequin Books S.A.

For questions and comments about the quality of this book,
please contact us at CustomerService@Harlequin.com.

Harlequin Enterprises ULC
22 Adelaide St. West, 40th Floor
Toronto, Ontario M5H 4E3, Canada
www.Harlequin.com

Printed in U.S.A.

USA TODAY bestselling author **Heidi Rice** lives in London, England. She is married with two teenage sons—which gives her rather too much of an insight into the male psyche—and also works as a film journalist. She adores her job, which involves getting swept up in a world of high emotions; sensual excitement; funny, feisty women; sexy, tortured men and glamorous locations where laundry doesn't exist. Once she turns off her computer, she often does chores—usually involving laundry!

Books by Heidi Rice

Harlequin Presents

Vows They Can't Escape
Captive at Her Enemy's Command
Bound by Their Scandalous Baby
Claiming My Untouched Mistress
Claimed for the Desert Prince's Heir

Conveniently Wed!

Contracted as His Cinderella Bride

One Night With Consequences

The Virgin's Shock Baby
Carrying the Sheikh's Baby

Visit the Author Profile page
at Harlequin.com for more titles.

To Teresa and Alan, the best hosts ever!

PROLOGUE

Belle

THE RIVIERA SUN blazed down as I stared into my best friend Remy Galanti's grave, but the sunshine did nothing to thaw the chill which had seeped into my bones over a week ago—ever since Remy's car had ploughed through the crash barrier at the Galanti test track in Nice and burst into flames. The horror of those moments played through my mind again, in agonising slow motion, but the tears wedged in my throat refused to fall.

I hadn't cried—for Remy, for myself, for his older brother, Alexi—because I couldn't. My body, like my mind, was numb.

The priest's voice droned on in French as I glanced across the grave to where Alexi stood.

He wore a dark linen suit and was surrounded by the local dignitaries and a host of celebrities and VIPs who had come out in force to show their respect to Monaco's—and motor racing's—foremost family at the loss of their second son. But as always Alexi looked utterly alone, his head bent and his stance rigid. A muscle in his jaw clenched and his dark hair was dishevelled, as if he had run his fingers through it a thousand times since the day we'd both watched Remy die.

His eyes, though, like mine, were dry.

Did he feel numb, the way I did? Destroyed by the loss of someone who had meant so much to us both? Remy had been my best friend ever since I had come to live in the Galanti mansion on the Côte d'Azur as a ten-year-old, when my mother had taken the job as the new housekeeper after Remy and Alexi's mother had run off to join one of her lovers.

I felt as if a part of my soul had been ripped out. But Alexi had lost a brother—the only person he had ever been close to after their mother's disappearance. Surely he had to be in as much distress as me, if not more?

But he didn't look numb as he glanced at the priest, his beautiful blue eyes sparking with impatience and contempt, he looked angry.

Not angry, furious.

Heat prickled over my skin, inappropriate but undeniable as the memories from a week ago played through my mind. The night before Remy's death the night when I'd thought every one of my dreams had come true—the night I had gone to Alexi and made love to him for the first time. I remembered the scent of salt and sweat and chlorine, the giddy rush of emotion, the glorious sensation of spending a few minutes in Alexi's strong arms and discovering what sex was all about.

Terrifyingly intimate but also fabulously exciting.

The brutal humiliation clutched at my heart as I stared at Alexi across the grave. He hadn't spoken to me since that night. I had tried to see him but he'd always been busy. Guilt pinched my ribs to go with the inappropriate heat that he always inspired in me, even at Remy's funeral.

Remy had always been there for me and now I wanted to be there for Alexi. I knew that was what Remy would have wanted. But still I felt guilty because I knew it wasn't just Remy's wishes I wanted to fulfil. But then Remy's final words to me replayed in my mind as the priest finished his graveside eulogy, the last of the words floating away on the gentle breeze scented with sea air and bougainvillea.

'My brother needs you, bellissima. *Alexi is lonely. He always has been. Just make me a promise,* bellissima. *Don't let him push you away. Okay?'*

The promise I had made to Remy rang in my head now as I watched Alexi pick up a fistful of dirt from the graveside and throw it onto the casket—his movements were stiff and lethargic, as if he had a weight on his shoulders he was struggling to bear. He looked so, so alone in that moment.

As the other mourners—many of whom had barely known Remy—lined up to drop dirt on the coffin, Alexi turned and walked towards the line of waiting limousines, ignoring the people offering their condolences.

Sending up a silent prayer for Remy as I glanced one last time at his coffin, I left the graveside and followed Alexi's retreating figure to the road out of the clifftop graveyard. For the first time since Remy's death the fog of shock and grief, the numbness, began to lift, the urgency allowing the adrenaline, the determination, to force the coldness out.

Breathless, I cried out as I saw him reach the lead car. 'Alexi, wait, please. Can we talk?'

He paused and turned, but his stance remained rigid. And, as I looked into them, his eyes were like shards of ice.

'Belle, what do you want?' The impatience shocked me, but not as much as the strident tone.

Was he angry with me? Was that why he had avoided me since Remy's death? But as soon as the thought occurred to me I dismissed it. I was being paranoid, insecure, and this was not the time. This wasn't about me, or about what we'd done seven nights ago. He wasn't angry with me. I simply didn't mean that much to him, I knew that, whatever Remy in his optimism had said about our liaison.

Alexi was angry at his brother's senseless death and probably furious with his father, who had arrived drunk at the funeral, not to mention angry at the fates who had robbed him of the last of his family—or the only part of his family who'd ever mattered to him.

He didn't want me sexually. He'd made that very clear after we'd slept together a week ago. It had been a mistake.

But that didn't mean I couldn't offer him friendship. If nothing more, I could offer him comfort in our shared grief, because I was the only other person who felt Remy's loss as keenly as he did.

'I wanted to make sure you're okay,' I said.

'Of course I'm not okay, I killed my brother.'

'*Wh...? What?*' The shiver at the coldness in his voice, and in his eyes, racked my whole body despite the warm day. Was he serious? How could he believe even for a moment he was to blame for Remy's death?

'You heard me,' he said, his anger slicing through my shock.

'But he wanted to be a driver, Alexi. It was his dream, his passion, for so long. You mustn't hold yourself responsible,' I said, trying to grasp the reason for his guilt.

Alexi had been managing the Galanti Super League team for two years now, ever since his father, Gustavo, had begun drinking so heavily he was no longer capable of hiding the extent of his addiction. Alexi had given Remy his chance as a test driver and had let him have his first lead this season. Was that why he blamed himself for Remy's accident?

He stared at me blankly, then his lips flattened into a grim line. 'Don't play the innocent with me. It won't work a second time.'

'I don't... I—I don't understand,' I stammered, the cynicism in his gaze chilling.

I hadn't bled when we had made love a week ago, even though Alexi was my first lover. I'd felt the pinch, the slight soreness, when he'd thrust heavily inside me—he wasn't a small man. But the pain had been so slight, so fleeting—the pleasure overwhelming in its intensity only moments later—that I was sure he hadn't realised about my virginity. At the time, I had been grateful. I didn't want him to think of me as a child. But when he spoke again I wasn't grateful any more.

'Stop playing the innocent. Remy knew what we'd done. He pretended it didn't matter, made some joke about it at the track that day before he went out, but you were always his girl. I should never have touched you. That's why he got distracted on the track, took the turn too fast.'

'But I... I was never Remy's girl, not like that. We were just friends,' I said, suddenly understanding where Alexi's guilt came from and wanting to make it right.

His eyebrows flattened, the muscle in his jaw jumped and the cynical twist of his lips sharpened as the chill in his blue eyes darkened.

'Was it you?' he hissed. 'Did you tell him we slept together even though I told you not to?'

'Yes,' I said, blurting out the truth.

I could have lied. A part of me wanted to lie—the agonising guilt in Alexi's eyes now fired by the light of fury—but I wasn't ashamed of what we'd done. Remy had been pleased about the possibility of us dating, not upset.

Alexi didn't understand about my friendship with Remy because he didn't know his younger brother was gay.

If only I could tell him that now. The truth lingered

on the tip of my tongue, but I couldn't voice it as I saw the pain behind the guilt in Alexi's eyes.

It would only hurt him more, to know Remy had confided in me and not him—and it had always been Remy's secret to reveal. If he'd wanted Alexi to know, wouldn't he already have told him? How could I break my confidence to Remy now, simply to save myself from his brother's wrath?

'Why did you tell him?' he asked, the accusation in his voice as raw as the pain.

'Because…' I stuttered to a stop.

Because Remy was gay, because we were friends, because he knew how much I had always loved you and he wanted us to be together.

But the words got stuck in my throat, behind the huge dam of emotion forged by the disgust etched on Alexi's face.

'Don't answer that,' he said before I could get the words out. 'I think we both know why you told him. Because you thought I was the better catch, didn't you? You figured, being the older brother, I was worth more.'

I was so stunned by his accusations I couldn't even begin to defend myself.

'You little whore. I knew I shouldn't have touched you, that it was wrong, but I never realised how wrong.'

His words were like physical blows—each one more painful than the last.

How could I ever have believed he loved me, cared about me, that he knew me at all, when he could accuse me of such things?

'I want you gone,' he said curtly. 'Out of my father's house. Today.'

'But…' I couldn't speak, couldn't even protect myself, the calmness in his voice almost as devastating as the flat, impersonal look in his eyes as the guilt, the anger, the bitterness, the cynicism all melted away and became nothing.

'I'll have the lawyers pay you off. I never want to see your face again.' He turned to climb into the car and I grasped his arm.

'Please, Alexi, don't do this. Don't shut me out,' I begged. 'You're hurting, you're in pain, I understand that, but so am I. We both loved Remy very much. Neither one of us is to blame for his death. It was a freak accident. We can get through this together.'

The bitter laugh shocked me to the core.

'We didn't love him. We killed him. Now we're both going to have to live with that betrayal. If I see you at the villa when I return, I'll have you arrested. You've got two hours to get your stuff together and leave. Send a forwarding address to my lawyers and I'll wire you a severance payment.'

He yanked his sleeve free. His gaze sliced over my figure and my body shuddered in an instinctive response that shamed me to my core even now.

'Don't worry, I'll be generous. Your hot little act on Friday night was worth at least a few thousand euro.'

I stood shaking as he climbed into the car and the long, black limousine pulled away from the curb then took the cliff road out of the cemetery. He didn't look back, not once.

The numbness returned, but this time it was all-consuming. The hollow ache in my insides became a black hole as the huge loss left by Remy's death combined with the agonising evidence that the dreams I'd had about Alexi ever since I'd hit puberty had always been a foolish schoolgirl's fantasy.

He wasn't the man I had believed him to be. The man I had adored from afar.

And he wasn't the man Remy had believed him to be either.

Alexi wasn't just reserved, or lonely, or simply wary of love. He was dead inside. Much deader than Remy could ever have been.

I walked down the path away from the cemetery and hailed a taxi to take me back to the Galanti estate where I had spent so much of my childhood.

But I didn't feel like a child any more. I felt about a thousand years old as I packed my belongings. It took me less than an hour before I was on the bus to Nice. I had some savings, enough to get me out of Monaco. I wasn't going to send Alexi's lawyer a forwarding address. I didn't want his money any more than I wanted him to know where I was.

I would return to London, I decided, my mind surprisingly calm. I had a second cousin there who might put me up if I begged. Since my mother's death two years ago, she was the only family I had left.

I needed to get away from Alexi, away from the agonising memories of my best friend, Remy, and the hole that would be left in my life for ever. I needed to leave the remnants of my girlhood behind me—

and the tattered remains of a dream that had never been real.

I'd loved Alexi for so long. I'd put him on a pedestal and idolised him. And when we'd finally made love I'd felt such passion, such excitement, in his arms.

But I'd never really known him. Not even while I had been clinging to his strong, powerful body and glorying in the feel of him inside me as he'd rocked us both to orgasm.

I knew him now, though. I knew his cynicism, his bitterness and his anger because I had become the target of all three.

'I'm so sorry, Remy,' I whispered as the bus made its way out of Monaco and along the coast road towards Nice. 'I couldn't keep my promise.'

The tears I had refused to shed flowed down my cheeks as Monaco's glittering lights disappeared behind the cliffs.

I scrubbed the tears away with my fist before any of the other passengers could see them, swallowed down the choking sobs making my ribs ache and kept my gaze on the road ahead.

At last, the numbness returned.

I embraced it this time, because it protected me from the agony threatening to consume me.

The numbness gave me strength.

A strength I would need to survive Remy's death—and Alexi's brutal rejection. And to find a new home, a new job and a new life far away from the Galantis.

CHAPTER ONE

Five years later

Alexi

'So who am I looking at and what's his price?' I squinted through my sunglasses at the track and adjusted my cap—which bore my rival Renzo Camaro's team logo—to ensure the bill covered my face as I spoke to Freddie Graham. Freddie was a freelance mechanic and an old friend. He'd given me the tip off twenty minutes ago that he'd spotted a fresh new talent driving Camaro's prototype at the Barcelona track as part of their testing for the new season.

I was desperate. Galanti's reserve driver, Carlo Poncelli, had just had a cancer diagnosis. We'd managed to keep it quiet for the last few days, but as soon as the news hit the circuit that Carlo was going to be receiving chemo treatment for most of the season every agent's price would go through the roof. I wanted to find someone quickly, someone talented and as yet undiscovered who would jump at the chance of getting a reserve seat in the Super League with the top team on the circuit—and was un-agented. It was a tall order, but if anyone could spot talent it was Freddie.

'Keep your voice down,' Graham said furtively as we watched the track together from the edge of the stands—out of sight of Camaro and his team. 'If Camaro finds out you're here checking out his employees, I'll get blacklisted.'

The noise of Camaro's new design drowned out the end of Freddie's sentence as the car came shooting round the bend and back into view. The car accelerated to two hundred miles an hour and the back wheels shuddered, but the driver brought it back under control with smooth, steely efficiency. The adrenaline rush I always got from watching a great new talent raised the hairs at my nape.

I would need to see stats and get a basic history before making an offer, find out the guy's age and what licences he held, but I already knew this was our man. I had a sixth sense about this stuff. It was what I was famous for on the circuit. Or rather, infamous for. That and having a different supermodel or actress on my arm at every event I attended.

'Who is he? Is he actually signed to Camaro yet? And why the hell haven't I heard of him?' I fired questions at Freddie as the car completed the circuit and headed into the pits.

If he was contracted to a team in one of the lower leagues, I'd have to buy him out, which would cost me. But I already knew I wanted him.

Camaro would probably have a cow. The guy was known for his hard business practices and the Destiny team had been Galanti's main rivals for three seasons. But if Renzo was only using this kid for test driving he was already missing a trick. I would have to act fast, though. We were already two months into the season. And I would need to get the new driver familiar with our car before winter testing.

'Slow down, fella,' Freddie said in his thick Brooklyn accent. 'Rumour on the track is she's one of Camaro's R&D people. She's not even a driver. Story is she's Renzo's mistress and he brought her over from London when his reserve driver got the flu. He needed someone to test the car, and he knows she's a talent, but when I saw her drive...'

Freddie's voice trailed off. But most of what he'd been saying had already washed over me because my brain had snagged on one word.

She.

This kid was a woman? *Dio!*

That was...

My mind exploded. That was an incredible PR opportunity. Even if I hadn't been desperate and she wasn't as good as she appeared I would have wanted to sign her.

There were female drivers in the lower leagues and on the reserve lists. Good female drivers who, sooner or later, would break into motor sport's top flight. But a female driver *this* good who was undiscovered and wasn't even attached to a team?

Except... My excitement downgraded.

She was attached to Renzo in a personal capacity.

'You say she's Renzo's mistress?' I turned to Freddie, his hangdog expression unchanged.

'That's what one of the mechanics told me. I saw them together and Renzo's all over her. Although she's a long way from being his usual type. She's kind of a tomboy.'

I frowned. Who knew Freddie was a gossip? But right now his nosiness suited my purposes. I wanted to know more about the girl before I approached her. If she was stuck on Renzo it might be a harder sell to get her to sign for me.

My lips quirked in a cynical smile.

'Whatever her connection to Camaro, I'm sure I can make her a better offer,' I said, confident any commitment she had to my rival could be broken.

She was a woman. Women in my experience could always be bought, with either money, orgasms or both. If I had to seduce her, I would. I wasn't dating anyone at the moment and I had no problem mixing business with pleasure. It was one of the perks of being a workaholic.

'Hold your jets, Casanova,' Freddie said. 'Renzo's not your only problem. The same mechanic told me she doesn't want to be a pro driver. Apparently Renzo's been trying to sign her to his young driver programme for over a year and she's not interested.'

'What? Why?' I couldn't hide my shock. Anyone with that much natural talent would be insane not to go for the gold ring. And no one could get that good in the first place without a passion for the sport.

'Haven't a clue. But I guess she must have her reasons.'

My surprise was quickly quashed by my confidence. Whatever her reasons, I'd figure out a way to overcome them. I knew how to play women, just like I knew how to play my rivals.

Charm was easy, seduction even easier. They were both commodities I'd learned to use to my advantage, deliberately honing my image as a womanising playboy to hide the ruthlessness that had driven me ever since Remy's death.

Thoughts of Remy killed the smile playing around my lips, reminding me not just of my boyish, reckless, stupidly trusting younger brother who had died so needlessly but also of the girl—*his* girl—who had screwed with my head far too often since Remy's death.

Belle Simpson had completely disappeared after Remy's funeral and I refused to give a damn about it. I'd tortured myself enough over the thought of her—soft, fresh and artlessly seductive—during that one night we'd shared. She'd been an illusion. She was no more pure and fresh than I was, or had ever been. Just because she'd never contacted me to get the pay off I'd offered her didn't make her innocent. Maybe her conscience had eventually got the better of her too, about what we'd both done to Remy.

I cut off the thought at the fresh slice of guilt. Remy was dead. I couldn't turn back the clock and undo what I'd done to him that night when Belle's wide emerald eyes had gazed at me as if I'd been everything she could ever want. That whole night had been screwed up. My cheek had been smarting from one of my father's back-handed slaps, my head fuzzy from one too many tequila slammers. I'd had to stop beating myself up for giving into the incendiary attraction between us.

I hated that, whenever I thought of Remy, I thought of her too. And her deep-green eyes wide with distress and unshed tears.

Ruthlessly pushing thoughts of my dead brother and that fateful night to one side, I bid goodbye to Freddie with the promise of a generous gift for his help if I managed to sign this girl.

I made my way towards the drivers' lounge behind the car hangars. Driving was hard, sweaty work, particularly in Barcelona in spring—the girl would have to shower and change before she did anything else. With the Camaro team cap pulled low, no one took any notice of me as I strolled past the team of mechanics busy assessing the new car's tyres for burn-out.

I spotted Camaro at the edge of the bay, talking to his chief mechanic, but no sign of the girl driver.

My hunch had been correct. She must have headed straight for the lounge area. Now all I had to do was hope my luck held out and I could catch her alone once she'd finished changing—to make her an offer she couldn't refuse.

Adrenaline pumped through my system. I'd always been a guy who revelled in the thrill of the chase—either in pursuit of a great new design, a talented driver or a beautiful woman. This girl could be a combination of all three.

The lounge area was empty. I noticed a makeshift sign stuck on one of the doors to the changing rooms reserved for individual drivers: *Solo Mujeres*.

Women only.

I almost laughed out loud as I sat down silently on one of the plush leather sofas.

Perfect—there was no one here. Giving me all the opportunity I needed to poach Renzo's mistress. And turn her into the driver she was meant to be. And maybe more.

I discarded the cap and the shades as I listened to the shower running in the adjoining changing room. And waited.

The shower eventually shut off and I could hear a soft British voice singing a French lullaby.

Something pricked at my consciousness. Why did the light, lilting voice sound so familiar?

Before I had a chance to register the question, the girl appeared in the doorway to the lounge, silhouetted by the bright sunlight shining through the windows behind her. She jolted and gasped, the sob of distress probably down to her surprise at finding a strange guy sitting in the lounge. I stood to introduce myself.

'Hi, Miss…' I paused, realising Freddie had never given me her name. 'I'm Alexi Galanti. I own and operate the Galanti team. We need a new reserve driver for the rest of the season and I want to offer you the position. Whatever Camaro's paying you, I'll double it.'

It was rash of me to offer her the job without talking to my legal team, getting her credentials properly checked out and giving her a probationary period. I couldn't even see her face properly and I hadn't heard her speak. Damn it, I didn't even know her name. But all my instincts were telling me to claim her, so I didn't regret the rash decision. I always trusted my instincts.

What I could see of her figure—her subtle curves seductively displayed in a pair of tomboy jeans and a white shirt and camisole—had my blood heating in my groin. Desire pumped through my veins with a visceral urgency.

Maybe it was the combination of hunger and desire combined with the knowledge of how she had handled Camaro's powerful car that was driving my determination—because I wasn't even sure what I wanted most any more. To see her in *my* car, or in my bed.

The hairs on the back of my neck prickled in time to the echo of the lullaby which still lingered in my mind as she stood silently, not speaking. I could hear her rapid, uneven breathing.

Something was wrong. Why was she so silent? So tense? Why was her stance strangely defensive, as if I'd insulted her instead of having offered her a million-dollar contract?

Then her scent invaded my nostrils—fresh, floral and disturbingly familiar, bringing back memories of the night five years ago that I had never been able to forget. Recognition struck me as she stepped into the light and her face was illuminated for the first time. The striking features—the soft, translucent skin, the sprinkle of girlish freckles across her nose, the sleepy emerald eyes and the wild shock of rich russet curls—were just as I remembered them from my dreams—and my nightmares. Grief, betrayal and longing arrowed into my gut to join the hot punch of lust that had never died.

'I don't want anything from you, Alexi,' she whispered, her voice a tortured rasp—both bold and defensive at the same time. 'I never did.'

CHAPTER TWO

Belle

IT WAS A lie. Once upon a time, I had wanted everything from Alexi Galanti. Not just his body, but his love. But as I stared at his tall, muscular body dressed in a T-shirt and worn jeans, the fabric stretched enticingly across pectoral muscles that had only become more defined in the last five years—not quite sure if he was real or a figment of my over-active imagination—I knew those desires were childish dreams borne of infatuation.

I'd locked those dreams away five years ago after the cruel banishment which had left me destitute, disillusioned and alone at nineteen.

And, as I'd discovered two months later, pregnant with his child.

I refused to let them resurface now just because he was even more handsome and compelling at thirty than he had been at twenty-five.

I was twenty-four now and I'd survived what he'd done to me. And I had a wonderful son whom I adored.

I struggled to quell the old yearning which shivered through me at the sight of him. A yearning I'd never been able to feel for any other man.

Heat careered into my cheeks as I watched him stiffen, the knowledge of who I was hitting him as hard as it had hit me a few moments before.

Good, I was glad. I wanted him to feel as raw as I did.

But, as soon as the ungenerous thought occurred to me, another horrifying realisation hit me—bringing with it the guilt I had struggled with for five years.

Oh, no! My cousin, Jessie, was bringing Cai—my son—to meet me at the track this afternoon.

I'd known it was a risk, agreeing to come to Barcelona to test drive the car I'd helped develop in my role as Camaro's fuel-efficiency expert for their R&D department in the UK. But Renzo, my boss, had been quite insistent and I had checked to make sure the Galanti team weren't scheduled to be at the test track today.

Cai loved the cars and the trip had been a special treat for him. But I didn't want him to come face to face with his father—or vice versa.

I'd never contacted Alexi to tell him about his son. I'd been in a daze, still struggling to cope with the loss of Remy, not to mention my job and my life in Monaco, when I'd discovered I was pregnant five years ago.

I hadn't had the courage or the strength to face Alexi then and as my pregnancy had progressed I had quickly begun to justify my cowardice to myself.

Alexi had made it very clear he hated me, that he blamed me for Remy's death. He'd told me he never wanted to see me again, that he'd have me arrested if he did. He'd called me a whore and implied I was a gold-digger. He probably wouldn't even have believed the child was his, so what would have been the point?

And, in the years since Cai's birth, it had become easier and easier not to make that call. My sweet, beautiful, smiley little boy, who looked so much like his father but would always be mine, would never know the cynicism, the coldness, of the man who had sired him. Really, I was just protecting my son.

I'd seen reports of Alexi's love life in the press, in gossip columns and celebrity blogs, over the intervening years too and had convinced myself Alexi wouldn't want to be a father. That I was doing him a favour by not divulging to him he had a son. Surely he wouldn't want to be tied down, to have his rampant womanising and glamorous social life hampered by a toddler?

But, now I was faced with the possibility of him meeting Cai for the first time, all my justifications began to crumble.

The guilt combined with the inappropriate yearning in the pit of my stomach made me plummet into the black hole I remembered from the last time I'd seen him—creating a wave of pure, unadulterated panic.

I'd always told myself that one day—when Cai was older, and I had become the foremost R&D specialist in the Super League and had some serious professional clout—I would get up the guts to inform Alexi of his son's existence.

But this wasn't that day. I wasn't ready to face that reality. Not yet. And neither was Cai. I hadn't prepared Cai for this news. And I doubted Alexi would even care if he had a son.

'I need you to leave,' I said, my voice firm, even though I was shaking inside from fear and the heat that would never die as long as I was in the same room as this man.

He hadn't said anything, he'd been rooted to the spot, but he controlled himself a lot faster than I did, the naked shock on his face masked by the cynical expression I remembered from our graveside parting. Although the heat in his gaze told another story, a heat I recognised from that fateful night when we had conceived Cai.

How could we still want each other when we both hated each other so much? I wondered vaguely, as my frantic mind tried to grasp the logistics of how I was going to avert the disaster galloping towards me with each tick of the clock.

Calm down, Belle, and don't show him any weakness.

I had twenty minutes. They weren't due here till three. I had time. All I had to do was get Alexi to leave before Jessie and Cai arrived. Surely it wouldn't be that hard, now he knew who I was? After all, he had been prepared to pay thousands of euros five years ago so he'd never have to see me again.

'The offer still stands,' he said at last.

'I… What? You can't be serious,' I said, stunned.

Surely he couldn't believe I would want to spend any time in his company, let alone work for him?

'I'm deadly serious. I need a reserve driver and I want you… You should be on the track, not behind it. Once you're signed with Galanti we can discuss the possibility of getting a full driver spot for you, maybe next season. I'll make it worth your while to break your attachment to Camaro…' His gaze dipped, his perusal swift but no less insulting, and the heat ignited in my cheeks as I saw the spark of desire and realised he thought Renzo and I were lovers.

I knew rumours were rife on the track and in the Camaro team that I was sleeping with the boss. Renzo had been instrumental in advancing my career, hiring me for his R&D team straight after I'd finished my masters in bioengineering and alternative fuel technology last year. He had been remarkably flexible about my childcare commitments on the job, had befriended Cai—who idolised him—and I did sometimes wonder if he thought of me as more than an employee and a friend… But he had never stepped over that line and I certainly hadn't encouraged him.

'I'm not for sale,' I said flatly, determined not to let my hurt at Alexi's insinuations show.

I didn't need this man's approval. It had taken me five years to get over his rejection. When I'd arrived in the UK and discovered I was carrying his child, the grief for Remy and everything I'd lost the day he'd died had all but destroyed me.

My confidence, and my sense of self had been left in tatters but I'd dragged myself up off the floor, with the help of my wonderful second cousin, Jessie, and forced myself to concentrate on what mattered.

I'd had my child and dedicated myself to supporting us both with two jobs, while taking on a mountain of student debt and studying late into the night to realise a new dream that in the last year had finally started to take off.

I had been a fool to keep the news of his child from him, something about which I had become starkly aware in the last few minutes. I would have to rectify that as soon as I could manage the news in a way that wouldn't hurt Cai.

But I didn't have to defend my professional reputation to Alexi or anyone else.

'That's a shame,' Alexi said, his husky voice sending goose bumps skittering over my skin. 'Because, whatever Renzo is paying you, you're worth more. And with the talent I saw on the track ten minutes ago it's obvious you should be driving.'

'I don't want to drive, not competitively,' I said, pushing past the sexual fog threatening to envelop me, to concentrate on getting him out of here. I didn't have time for a negotiation. Or to obsess over the way he could still make me feel simply by looking at me.

Why did I have to be so affected by this man? It was as if a spell had been cast on me as soon as I'd hit puberty and I couldn't escape the enchantment of my own body.

So not the point, Belle.

'Why the hell don't you want to drive?' Alexi shot back, his frustration only making his dark good looks and intense gaze all the more overwhelming. 'That was always your dream ever since you were a kid, wasn't it?'

I was surprised he had remembered that much about me. As a teenager, and later as a man, he had always made a point of ignoring me. Until that night.

'It was my dream *once*,' I said. 'It's not my dream any more. Now, would you please leave before I call security?' It was an empty threat, and we both knew it. No security guy in his right mind would eject Alexi Galanti from the track—the man was motor-racing royalty. But I was desperate.

Not surprisingly, he ignored the threat and, instead of leaving, stepped closer. Close enough for me to capture his intoxicating scent—spice, musk and the hint of pine soap. The aroma made my knees shake, propelling me back to that night—somewhere I *so* did not need to go ever again.

I stood my ground, though, because showing Alexi a weakness had never ended well.

'Tell me why,' he insisted, the frustration disappearing to be replaced with something much more disturbing—genuine interest in me and my life, something I'd yearned for all through my teenage years. 'Tell me why you gave up on your dream, *bella notte*,' he repeated, his voice soft, coaxing, as he used the nickname he had coined that night, no doubt to intimidate me more. 'And then I'll leave.'

I opened my mouth, determined to give him an answer, any answer that would make him leave and take this pointless yearning away again. But the only explanation I could think of was the real one.

Because I have a child, a son, who I love more than life itself. And I'm the only person he has. I can't risk leaving him alone—dying the way Remy died. So I found a way to readjust my dreams. To feed my passion for racing—while also fulfilling my obligations to my child.

But I couldn't tell him that.

As I racked my brains, trying to come up with a viable alternative reason Alexi would believe, it occurred to me I'd been hoisted by my own dishonesty.

And then the door burst open and Cai ran into the room ten minutes early, a four-year-old bundle of energy…and the black hole in the pit of my stomach imploded. For the first time in my life I was not pleased to see him.

My time had run out.

'Mummy, Mummy, I saw the car!' he cried, practically bursting with excitement as he raced towards me, oblivious to Alexi and everything else. 'Mr Renzo let me touch it.'

He ran past Alexi, who stepped back, his dark brows launching up his forehead. Cai's sturdy body barrelled into me and the love I had felt for him as soon as I'd held him in my arms after ten agonising hours of labour washed through me.

'Mr Renzo said I could sit in it if I'm good.'

Cai's arms wrapped around my legs as he peered up at me, the love in his eyes all-consuming and utterly uncomplicated. The blue of his irises was the same true, iridescent aquamarine as those of the man standing two feet away, staring at him as if he were an alien.

'Can I, Mummy? Can I?' he pleaded, completely oblivious to the tension now snapping in the room. I could almost feel Alexi's mind working as he stared at my child and calculated dates and ages. Cai was tall for a four-year-old, probably because his father was six-foot-three, but that wasn't going to help me.

With the light from the window shining onto Cai's dark, wavy hair and illuminating his face and his Galanti bone structure—which had become more defined in the last year or two as he'd grown from toddlerhood into boyhood—the resemblance to his father was all the more striking.

Alexi was not a stupid man, and as my gaze connected with his over Cai's head I watched as he figured out Cai's heritage—the stunned disbelief turning to shock before a sharp frown flattened his brows and his sensual lips pursed into a tight line of accusation.

'Can I, Mummy?'

My gaze dropped back to Cai, my thoughts in turmoil as my heart rammed my tonsils. I ruffled his silky hair, trying to stop my hand shaking. I needed to get my son out of here, away from Alexi. I didn't want Cai to witness our impending confrontation. Whatever else I knew, I knew this was not his fault.

'Of course you can, Cai-baby,' I said, using the nickname which always made him giggle.

'I'm not a baby any more, Mummy. I'm a big boy.' The infectious laughter—so innocent, so delighted—

only tightened the knots of anguish in my stomach. Whatever happened next, my only thought now had to be to protect my child from the fallout of this revelation.

I knelt down so I could hold Cai and momentarily shield myself from the accusatory frown of the man standing behind him.

'Yes, but have you been a good boy?' I asked.

Cai nodded furiously. 'Yes, Mummy. Ask Auntie Jessie, she'll tell you, I had my nap without making any fuss at all.'

'Is that true, Jess?' I asked my cousin, who had entered the lounge behind Cai and was glancing backwards and forwards between Alexi and his child.

I'd never told Jessie who Cai's father was—and she knew nothing about motor racing, so she wouldn't recognise my former employer—but it was obvious she had noticed the resemblance.

'I wouldn't say *no* fuss,' she said, letting out a nervous half-laugh. 'But certainly minimal fuss. Shall I take Cai back to the car hangar and see if he can sit in the car yet?' she added, sizing up the situation.

Thank you, Jessie. You are my life saver. Again.

I nodded. 'Great.' I cleared my throat, my voice breaking on the word, my gratitude for all this woman had done for me and Cai over the last five years choking me. 'I'll join you in a minute.'

At least whatever I had to face with Alexi now would not be faced in front of Cai.

'Yes!' Cai jumped up and punched the air, his face beaming with triumph and happiness. 'Come soon, Mummy, I want you to see me sit in the car too. And take pictures to show Imran,' he said, mentioning his best friend at pre-school.

He went to run to Jessie but stopped abruptly, noticing Alexi for the first time. 'Hello,' he said with the confidence of a four-year-old who had never learned to be intimidated by anything. 'Are you my mummy's friend?'

Alexi stared at his son without speaking, and the guilt which I had tried so hard not to acknowledge for so long all but overwhelmed me.

Had I done a terrible thing, not contacting Alexi? I wondered as I watched Alexi's gaze roam over his son's features, absorbing every detail.

'Yes,' Alexi said at last, lifting his gaze from Cai to me, his voice a rasp of emotion.

The slow-burning judgement in his eyes— judgement I recognised from all those years ago by Remy's graveside—made it clear that was a lie.

He wasn't my friend. He was my adversary.

Thankfully Cai didn't notice the harsh look as he rushed to join Jessie. But he stopped at the door and turned back, gifting Alexi one of his sunniest smiles. 'You can come too and see me sit in the car if you like.'

Alexi nodded. 'Okay.'

Jessie ushered Cai out of the room, sending me a concerned look. 'Take as long as you need,' she said.

It occurred to me that for ever might not be long enough as the door shut behind them. I had brought this on myself. Now I had to negotiate a way out of it. But was that even possible?

The silence descended like a shroud as I waited

for the axe to fall but, when Alexi spoke, he said the last thing I had expected.

'Your son's resemblance to Remy is remarkable. Why the hell didn't you tell me you were carrying his child when I kicked you out?'

For a moment I was confused, but then I remembered the accusation Alexi had flung at me at the graveside—that I had cheated on Remy, that we both had. That Remy and I had been *more* than friends… that we had been lovers.

For another moment, I considered letting Alexi believe that misconception. If I told him Cai was Remy's child, he would have no real claim on my son. On *our* son.

But it only took a moment more for the mushroom cloud of guilt I had denied for so long to halt that line of reasoning.

There had been so many lies between us and so many omissions. I had kept Remy's sexuality a secret for five years, just like the secret of our son's existence, and it had brought us both to this point.

I had to tell Alexi the truth now, however hard. No more excuses.

'He doesn't look like Remy, Alexi. I never slept with your brother. *You* were my first lover…' *My only lover*, I almost added, but bit into my lip to stop that truth coming out.

Alexi didn't need to know no other man had ever made me feel the way he had. The way he could still make me feel if the heat pulsing deep in my abdomen was anything to go by.

I needed to tell him the truth now—but never again did I intend to make myself as vulnerable as I had been before. And my sexual history—or lack of it—was none of his business.

'Cai's not Remy's son...' I continued, because he looked suspicious now as well as confused, the brittle cynicism turning his features to stone. I took a deep breath, forcing myself to continue. 'He's not your brother's son, Alexi. He's yours.'

CHAPTER THREE

Alexi

I STARED AT Belle, stunned by her revelation.

I had known, as soon as the child had run into the room and grasped his mother's legs, that the boy was a Galanti. His round, open face, thick thatch of dark curls and sunny demeanour as he'd bombarded his mother with questions and requests had been so like Remy at the same age, it had been like seeing a ghost.

A ghost of the brother I'd lost, the brother I still missed, the only person who had ever really known me.

Shock had come first, but my surprise had quickly been overcome by the rush of an emotion I couldn't name and, more terrifyingly, couldn't control. It was sharp like the grief, loss and guilt which had dogged me for five years but was tangled up with joy—the joy of seeing that happy, uncomplicated face I'd thought I would never see again once more.

Not Remy's child, *my* child. That was what she'd said. But I didn't believe her. Or, rather, I didn't want to believe her.

How could this child be mine? I was not a father, could never be a father, did not deserve to be a father.

How did I know she wasn't lying? She said I'd been her first, but how could that be when she and Remy had been like each other's shadows ever since her mother had first come to work for us? Remy had loved her, that much I did know. But...

The desire which had been lurking rippled through me as I recalled the intense physical connection of our one night together—the feel of soft skin, her staggered sobs as I'd entered her, the riot of pleasure cascading through me as I came...inside her.

I hadn't used a condom—hadn't been sober enough or smart enough to think about it. And the next day, when I had intended to check on her, Remy's crash, his death, had made me forget everything except my guilt at taking his girl, at using her to salve my own loneliness...

I dragged a hand through my hair and studied her face, trying to get my thoughts in order and quell the rioting pulse of emotion, the relentless desire for her, that was still there despite everything.

Did it really matter which one of us had fathered the child? If he was a Galanti I needed to protect him, give him the family name, make him my heir. And find out why she had not told me of his existence until now.

Had she ever intended to tell me?

Her face was a picture of stubborn integrity, but I could see the flicker of guilty knowledge in her eyes.

My usual cynicism returned full force. What was

I thinking? Of course she hadn't told me the truth about the boy's parentage. The same reasons she had come on to me that night still applied. I had no evidence of the innocence she claimed. Had she bled? I was fairly certain she had not. Although I'd been too ashamed of my own actions, the shocking pleasure of our union, to be absolutely sure.

One thing was certain, though. She had responded to me with an intensity that had taken my breath away. I still had dreams about her soft, breathy sobs as her body had contracted around mine, forcing me to a climax so staggering that just the echo of it had woken me up on so many nights since then, sweaty and desperate, my groin aching, my erection as hard as iron.

Was that normal for a novice? How would I know? I'd never been a woman's first before. Had certainly never wanted that responsibility. And I didn't want it now. So I rejected her claims in favour of the narrative I had settled on five years ago.

'Seriously? You expect me to believe you never slept with Remy?' I said, my voice carefully devoid of the emotions churning in my stomach and tightening my ribs.

She blinked, stiffened, the flicker of distress in the green depths quickly masked but there nonetheless.

What the hell? Was she really that easy to read? Or was she simply a consummate actress?

'I'm telling you I know Cai is your son, not Remy's—whether you believe it or not is up to you.'

She went to walk past me but I grasped her arm,

the emotion thundering so hard against my ribs now that the struggle to control it—to stop her from seeing it—was impossible. I couldn't stay here. I needed to get away, to think, to clear my head and decide what needed to be done now. And most importantly of all regain the emotional equilibrium that had become an integral part of who I was since my brother's death.

'There's a simple way to find out the truth. I want a DNA test done,' I said.

I needed to know. Was the boy mine or my brother's? Once I had the full facts at my fingertips, I could begin to figure out how I was going to deal with this staggering revelation.

She tugged her arm out of my grasp. I could see she hadn't expected that demand. I could also see she wanted to refuse the request.

Satisfaction and a strange sense of regret powered through me.

I was right. I had not been her first. She didn't know if the child was mine or Remy's. Why else would she want to avoid a DNA test? Either she knew the boy was Remy's or she didn't know which of us had fathered her child.

For all I knew, she might have slept with us both that day.

The memory of her face from five years ago, so open, giving and compassionate, flashed before me. I dismissed it. Just another lie. Another act.

She blinked furiously, as if close to tears, but then her chin firmed and she stared back at me.

'Okay,' she said, surprising me with her capitulation. Clearly she had decided to gamble with the possibility I *was* the boy's father.

I wasn't sure how I felt about that, the emotions confusing me again.

Did I secretly want to be the child's father? How could that be true when I'd never intended to become a parent? When I knew Remy had always been the best of us. That it would be much better if he could claim this legacy now not me.

I shut down the foolish rush of yearning that the boy was mine.

It made no sense. And, anyway, until I had the results of the test, I did not have to deal with this confusing tangle of emotions.

'But I want it conducted discreetly,' she said. 'And I don't want my son to know what's going on until…'

She glanced down at her hands. They were clasped together, the knuckles white. 'Until I've had a chance to prepare him,' she finished, releasing her fingers and shoving her open hands into the back pocket of her jeans.

She forced her chin up to meet my gaze.

The defiant yet oddly defensive stance pressed her breasts against the soft cotton of her camisole.

I bit into my lip, determined not to let the inevitable endorphin-rush distract me. And found myself drowning in those mossy eyes when our gazes met, the way I had all those years ago.

Damn it, Galanti, snap out of it. She's an actress and a gold-digger.

But with her face devoid of make-up she looked

so young, as young as she had been that night, still a
teenager, and it was harder to make myself believe it.
I could see the sprinkle of freckles across her nose,
could remember her sweet sighs as I kissed every one
of them before devouring those plump lips which had
tasted of cherry cola and eagerness.

'Once you have the proof you need, what do you
intend to do?' she asked.

I frowned at the direct question, the guilelessness
of it disturbing me. Until I got a grip.

*It's just an act. She looks artless, innocent, but
she's playing you. No one is ever really honest.
There's always an agenda. Once you've found out
exactly what her agenda is, you'll be back on solid
ground again.*

Obviously it made no sense that she would keep
the boy's existence a secret from me for five years,
and had never contacted me for the severance cheque,
if this was a simple case of extortion.

But maybe her agenda was more sophisticated than
that. Was she playing a longer game, to get more? And
why did I really care anyway? As long as I took control
of the situation, it didn't matter what her agenda was,
because my agenda was the one that would prevail.

'I don't know,' I replied, even though I knew what
I wanted was likely to conflict with what she wanted.

*Never show your hand until you are ready to play
your cards.*

It was a motto I had lived by for a long time. It
had won me considerable amounts at the high-stakes
game in my friend Dante Allegri's casino and had

also been a guiding principle in my business and personal life.

'I wasn't expecting to find out I had a four-year-old son today,' I said.

Or that Remy had one, I added silently to myself, even though that strange yearning for the boy to be mine was still pulsing in my chest. I'd figure that out later too. 'Once I have the information, I'll be in touch.'

Whatever the outcome of the DNA test, I planned to claim the child as a Galanti. And punish her for not having told me of the boy's existence a lot sooner. I also planned to have her thoroughly investigated.

Is she sleeping with Renzo?

The question popped into my head as something wholly unfamiliar tore through my insides. Something visceral and indiscriminate. I had to curl my fingers into fists to stop me from acting on the sudden urge to capture her face in my hands and claim those lush lips with my own—driving my tongue into the recesses of her mouth until she clung to me the way she had before and I plunged deep into her....

I tensed and shoved my fists into the pockets of my jeans, shocked by the direction of my thoughts.

Dio, I needed to get laid. Clearly the shock of seeing the child, of seeing her again, had had an unpredictable effect not just on my emotional equilibrium but on my libido.

I was off-kilter, not a condition I was used to, which explained this forceful and inexplicable reaction.

She nodded, apparently taking my answer at face value.

'I… I understand,' she said.

No, you don't, but you will.

Whatever the result of the DNA test, she had kept the child's existence from me for five years. And for that she would pay.

'I should go,' she said, strangely polite. 'Cai is waiting for me. Let me know what you need and when for the test. I think it's just a swab. I can make it into a game to explain it to Cai.' She huffed out a breath to stop the babble of information, but her nervousness was visible in her trembling fingers as she pushed the shock of ruddy curls away from her face.

This was not an act. But then, if she had any idea what I was thinking, she had a lot to be nervous about.

'I'll… I'll speak to you again about Cai, when you're ready,' she said.

Walking over to the sofa, she picked up a large bag, rummaged inside and produced a card. 'This is my work number. I'll…we'll…be back in the UK by tomorrow night. And you can contact me there most week days between nine and five. Or my PA will take a message.'

She handed me the card and our fingers brushed. I managed to stifle the sudden jolt of reaction. Her, not so much.

Why did that make me want to smile, despite everything?

The tug of amusement died, though, as I read the

address on her business card and recognised the location of Camaro's R&D headquarters in London.

The surge of possessiveness was as visceral as that strange pulse of jealousy and lust, but I explained it to myself as I watched her sling her purse over her shoulder.

I might be unclear at the moment about how much of a father—or an uncle—I was capable of being to this child. But he would need to live in Monaco, to understand his Galanti heritage. And that would mean his mother would have to come too.

It would be no hardship offering her a position in our R&D operation, if her credentials were as good as Freddie had suggested, and I did still need a reserve driver. That situation hadn't changed from when I'd first walked into this room. Even if everything else had.

'Goodbye, Alexi,' she said. 'I'm sorry…' She paused, her regret looking surprisingly genuine. 'I'm sorry I didn't tell you about Cai sooner. That was wrong of me. Call me when you're ready.'

I nodded as the emotion I'd been keeping so carefully at bay swelled against my ribs.

I watched her disappear back into the changing area, probably to collect her racing suit. I strode out of the lounge area. The emotion threatened to choke me as I headed towards the track's parking lot and away from the car hangars where the boy was with his babysitter.

You need to take stock, to know exactly what you're dealing with before you proceed.

But, even as the mantra ran through my head, all the conflicting emotions churned in my stomach: grief, longing, desire, anger, confusion. My fingers shook as I fished my key out of my pocket and clicked the fob.

As I climbed into the car, fired up the engine and drove away, I knew my whole life had changed in the space of one afternoon. The reality of that fact was reinforced by the tug of something vivid and inescapable—was it lust, regret, longing or grief? Who the hell knew?

But the force of it was dragging me back into the past harder than the G-force in the driver's seat of our newest model when it hit two hundred miles per hour.

I had been running from myself, and my sins against Remy, for five years, maybe longer, and now the truth of what I'd done, what we'd both done to him, had caught up with me.

In the shape of one boisterous little boy and a woman I had never been able to forget—unlike any other, even my own mother—even though I had tried.

CHAPTER FOUR

Belle

Dear Mlle Simpson

The results of the test carried out on May 20th by The Royal Harley Street Clinic on the DNA of your son, Cai Remy Simpson, and Mr Alexi Gustavo Galanti show a 99.98 percentage probability that he is the father of your child.

As a result of this information, Mr Galanti has asked me to inform you that he has arranged for you to fly out to Monaco on his private jet on May 23rd for a meeting with him, myself and the rest of his legal team at Villa Galanti so we can outline how he plans to proceed.

I enclose details of the travel arrangements and your overnight stay at the villa.

A car will collect you at your home address at ten that morning.

Salutations distinguées,

Etienne Severo, avocat

I READ THE email from Alexi's lawyer which had arrived while I'd been busy packing Cai's lunch box and trying to cajole him into putting on his shoes that morning.

I hadn't had time to panic about it then, but I had lots of time to panic about it now as I read it for the five-thousandth time.

I hadn't done any work this morning. My fear at the curt demand choked me. Alexi expected me to drop everything and come to Monaco to find out how *he* planned to proceed in two days' time. And to stay overnight at Villa Galanti. He'd given me virtually no time to arrange leave or childcare, and there had been little mention of Cai. While I was grateful he hadn't asked me to bring Cai, the impersonal nature of the solicitor's letter, and the laying down of battle lines contained within it, disturbed me.

I had expected Alexi's high-handed, dictatorial approach. Of course he mistrusted me. I'd kept his son's existence from him, and what evidence did he have I would ever have told him but for a chance encounter? But in the last few days I had hoped that, once Cai's parenthood was established, he would contact me personally—that his first priority would be getting to know the innocent four-year-old child at the centre of this situation.

I read the email again, scanning it for any evidence of warmth or empathy towards his son. Even if I didn't deserve any sympathy, surely Cai did? But the words remained as cold and compassionless as when I'd first read them.

A prickle of anger burned under my breastbone,

which made an unfortunate bedfellow for the panic which had consumed me all morning.

Part of me wanted to refuse his demand. I didn't want to go to the Galanti mansion—there were so many memories there waiting to hijack me—and demanding I go alone and stay the night at the villa could only be a ploy to unsettle and unnerve me.

I closed the email app on my phone as the anger fizzled out.

Whatever Alexi's agenda was, and however scared I was about the outcome of this 'meeting', I couldn't keep running away from the confrontation I had avoided for so long. I had hoped Alexi would be reasonable. Clearly that wasn't going to happen, but I owed it to my son to hear what his father had to say.

I could feel Alexi's anger with me in the lawyer's words. And I had to face that in order to move forward now.

Because I'd seen how confused, how emotional, Alexi had been when I'd revealed Cai's identity to him nearly a week ago. Even though he'd tried exceptionally hard to hide it, I had blindsided him.

And I had to accept he had a right to be angry with me.

I dialled Jessie's number. My cousin picked up on the first ring.

'Hey, Belle,' she said, her warm voice already helping to release the pressure which had been strangling me ever since my fateful meeting with Alexi—a pressure which had become unbearable ever since his lawyer's email had arrived.

'Hi, Jess. I need to go to Monaco day after to-morrow and stay overnight… Could you look after Cai while I'm gone? I know it's super-short notice and I—'

'Don't be daft,' Jessie interrupted. 'You know I love to look after him. What time do you need me there?'

I rattled off the details.

Cai hadn't done anything wrong, even if I had. Cai's welfare always came first—and if Alexi's 'plans' for me and our son turned out to be not in Cai's best interests I would tell him so.

I didn't like the implication in the lawyer's email that Alexi planned to tell me how he was going to handle this situation and I would just be expected to follow his orders. But it shouldn't surprise me.

Alexi had always been pushy and, well, frankly domineering and determined to get his own way. He'd been like that ever since I'd first known him as a teenager on the rare occasions when he'd deigned to notice the housekeeper's infatuated daughter, so it was no surprise he was even more of a dictator now.

I had toyed with the idea of hiring a lawyer to ac-company me to Villa Galanti but had decided against it. Why make this even more confrontational than it already was? I would not be signing anything at this meeting, and he couldn't force me to do so, because I was now the opposite of that infatuated teenager.

So I would go to Monaco, to his meeting, listen politely to what he had to say, deal with his anger, his enmity and his legal team and then, once I returned to the UK, I would hire my own lawyer to thrash out the child custody arrangements.

The anxiety thrummed under my breastbone again.

I earned a very good salary from Camaro. But I still had student loans to pay, not to mention Cai's childcare and a large mortgage for our tiny flat in west London. I wouldn't be able to afford a legal team anywhere near as fancy as Alexi's… I took a steadying breath.

Don't go getting ahead of yourself.

I didn't even know yet what he wanted to do. It was quite possible he wouldn't even want any custody. He hadn't exactly seemed overjoyed at the news he had a son. Just stunned, wary and then angry. I might well be panicking about nothing. Perhaps this meeting was simply to punish me for not telling him about his child.

'Why are you going to Monaco? Is it a work thing?' Jessie's calming voice drew me back to the present before the panic started to choke me again.

'Sort of,' I attempted to lie, but my response didn't sound convincing even to me. I had always been a terrible liar.

'It's not to do with Alexi Galanti, then?' Jessie's question had my belly knotting.

'How do you know about him?' I rasped.

'I looked him up after he freaked you out so much in Barcelona.'

'Right,' I said. I thought I'd managed to hide that from Jessie. 'So you noticed that, huh?'

'Yes, I noticed that, Belle. I also noticed his resemblance to Cai. Is he his father?' She'd never asked me the question before, and I'd been pathetically grateful for that over the years, but I could see now that was just more evidence of what a coward I'd been. Jessie had a right to know. She'd helped me get back on my feet when I'd turned up on her doorstep pregnant, destitute and distraught.

'Yes, he is,' I said.

'And I'm assuming he knows that too, if he's an observant man.'

Alexi was certainly that. 'He insisted on a DNA test.' His mistrust still stung, but I was trying to make that not about me.

Alexi had never really trusted anyone, especially not women, not since his mother had run away and left his brother and him alone to deal with their alcoholic father.

'The results came through from his lawyer this morning,' I continued. 'He's arranged for me to fly to Monaco to talk about his plans.'

'*His* plans?' Jessie asked. 'That sounds arrogant.'

'You have no idea,' I murmured. 'I'm scared. I have no idea what he's planning to tell me, but I doubt it will be pleasant. I'm scared he's so angry with me he might try to use Cai to get back at me,' I added, finally voicing my real fear.

Alexi still believed I was a gold-digger and a whore, a woman who had cheated on his brother and lied to protect herself. Who got ahead by using men and then discarding them. A woman who had no loyalty, no honour and no morals. Given that I'd only ever slept with him, his low opinion of me would almost be funny if it weren't so damning and… I swallowed sharply, finally forced to admit something else…hurtful. It shamed me to realise Alexi's low opinion still had the power to hurt me when Cai's feelings were the only thing that mattered now.

'What makes you think he'll do that?' Jessie asked, sounding shocked and a little scared too. If she'd investigated Alexi at all she had to know how rich he was, and how powerful.

'Well, mostly the fact that he demanded to see me, but not Cai. I'm not even sure if he wants to be a father. He hardly mentions Cai in the letter.'

'Okay.' Jessie sighed, sounding relieved. 'Perhaps that's not all that surprising, though.'

'How so?' I asked.

'He's a billionaire playboy who seems to have a revolving-door policy with girlfriends.' Okay, so Jessie had *really* checked him out. 'What does he know about the needs of a four-year-old? Or being a father, for that matter? He's clearly super-arrogant but he doesn't strike me as a stupid man. Perhaps he's simply asked to see you alone first so he can get a better handle on being a dad.' She coughed. 'As well as give you hell for keeping Cai a secret for so long…' Jessie's voice trailed off into silence, but I could hear the soft note of censure. She'd never asked me about the circumstances of Cai's parentage, because I'd always made it clear to her I didn't want to discuss it, but I could hear the question in her tone now even if she hadn't asked it.

Why had I done it?

'Belle, you're not scared of him for any other reason, are you?' she asked gently. 'He didn't hurt you, did he? Force you in any way? That isn't why you ran, is it? Why you didn't want him to know about his son?'

'God, no!' I rasped as the shame cascaded through me.

'Are you sure?' she probed again.

'Yes, it wasn't like that,' I said, but the tightening in my throat made it hard for me to speak as every detail of our encounter flooded back—hot, febrile and exciting, but never frightening.

And I finally had the real answer why I was so scared to return to Villa Galanti and face Alexi alone. It wasn't just because of the hostile reception I knew I would face from him. It wasn't fear of what plans he might have for Cai's custody or even his motivations behind them. It was the harsh truth that my desire for him had never died and spending two days and one night in his company—at the location of my original downfall—had the potential to bring all those needs and wants hurtling back.

It was terrifying to realise the girl I thought had been lost long ago might still be lurking inside me somewhere, still yearning for Alexi's touch…and his affection.

As the helicopter circled Villa Galanti, the emotions rushing towards me were as strong, if not stronger, than the downdraft from the blades.

Nothing could have prepared me for the hard hit of grief as the big black machine drifted over the estate's private beach and the landscaped gardens. The marble statues and elegant follies, the enchanting water features and ancient woods, the beds overflowing with shrubs and flowers, all morphed into pirate ships, cowboy forts and haunted hideouts in my mind's eye as I imagined Remy and I running through them together as children and then teenagers.

As the helicopter flew over the fifteen-bedroomed Belle Époque mansion at the centre of the estate, and the small housekeeper's cottage behind where I had lived with my mother, the villa's swimming pool on the garden's lower terrace came into view.

My already pounding heart jumped into my throat then sunk deep into my abdomen as another memory blazed through my body. The blast of heat made my thighs tremble and my nipples pebble into hard peaks.

I had known my mind and my body would play tricks on me, but as I stared at the marble pool below, the sunshine glinting off the crystal-blue water, the whirring blades making the palm trees ruffle and bend, I knew I hadn't factored in the power of those recollections as they reared out of my subconscious and struck me like a bolt of lightning, searing and devastating…

My heartbeat accelerated as I imagined myself, aged nineteen in the green cocktail dress I had donned after I had spotted Alexi heading towards the pool terrace…and raced after him…

* * *

My heart rammed into my throat as I crept past the pool house, the sultry night air settling around me like a blanket. My gaze landed on the pool perched on the clifftop overlooking the sea. The underwater lighting gave the water a turquoise glow and illuminated the even more breathtaking figure of a man slicing through the pool in powerful, efficient strokes.

I stumbled back to shield myself, my eyes going so wide it was a wonder my eyeballs didn't pop right out of my skull.

My heart swelled, beating so hard and fast it started to gag me.

Was Alexi naked? I wondered as I spotted a pile of clothes on one of the loungers. I studied his strong shoulders, powerful arms and tanned back ploughing through the water and tried to focus on what lay beneath the surface.

The butterflies in my stomach formed into a boulder. A hot, heavy boulder that got wedged between my thighs and made my sex beat with the same furious, erratic rhythm as my heart.

The figure powered to the end of the pool then executed a perfect backflip to thunder back towards me.

I spotted his boxer shorts clinging to the bunched muscles of his backside.

Not naked.

My galloping heartbeat slowed. A little. And my breath gushed out of constricted lungs.

But my relief was short lived when Alexi levered

himself out of the pool only a few feet from where I stood.

I flattened myself against the wall, trying to be invisible as the water cascaded off his broad shoulders. He stood on the pool patio, the wet boxers clinging to the long muscles of his flanks as he scooped up a towel from the lounger. Water glistened on his tanned skin in the moonlight as he scrubbed his hair, making it stick up in tufts.

I should have left, given him his privacy. But I stood transfixed, trapped by the sensations rioting through my body as he slung the towel around his neck, slid his thumbs under the waist band of his wet shorts and bent to shove them down his legs. He kicked them off and straightened, rubbing the towel over his groin.

My heart hammered my ribs so hard it was a miracle I didn't pass out.

Alexi Galanti naked was more beautiful than anything I could ever have imagined. And I'd imagined a lot.

He stood silhouetted against the pool glow and the twinkle of lights from Monte Carlo across the bay, spotlighted like Adonis against the night.

No, not Adonis.

Poseidon.

This was not a boy. This was a man. A god-like man.

He flung down the towel and reached for his jeans, leaving him standing completely naked in front of me. I could see absolutely everything now.

Oh. My. Good. God.

My breath released in a shattered gasp.

His head shot up and he pinned me with that searing blue gaze. Heat exploded in my cheeks like a volcano, the hot lava of mortification spreading over my face and flooding across my collarbone.

He held his clothing over his groin, his dark brows drawn in a sharp frown. But he didn't look embarrassed, just annoyed.

'Belle, what the hell do you think you're doing? Go back to bed.'

My humiliation threatened to engulf me at the curt command—but, before I could mumble my way through an apology and flee, something Remy had said to me recently echoed in my skull.

Alexi wants you too. He's just better at hiding it.

And suddenly I noticed the tension in his jaw and the flicker of something dangerous in those impossibly blue eyes.

Was I imagining Alexi's response, thanks to years of adolescent fantasies and the massive sensory overload I had just endured? But, even if that was true, did it matter?

If I wanted Alexi to stop treating me like a child, I had to stop acting like one. I gathered every ounce of courage I had ever possessed and stepped out of the shadows and into the moonlight, close enough to smell the chlorine on his skin and see the ripple of tension make his pectoral muscles quiver.

'No,' I said, a little astonished by how clear my voice sounded when I was dying inside.

If he rejected me now, if he treated me like a child,

if Remy had been wrong, I might never recover. But somehow I knew—just like Remy, when he pressed his foot to the floor and let the new Galanti prototype soar—that the possible reward was worth the risk.

'What do you mean, no?' Alexi replied, the dark frown arrowing down so sharply I could almost see thunderclouds forming above his head.

'I'm not going to bed.' I let my gaze glide over the planes and angles of his body, let the lava settle between my thighs. The scatter of scars from the many times his father had hurt him added to the deep well of compassion in my ragged breathing. 'I want to be here, with you. I'm not a child any more, Alexi.'

He blinked slowly, his beautiful lips, the lips I'd yearned to feel on mine so many times, firming into a thin line. A new wave of heat raged through me.

But this wasn't embarrassed heat any more. It was excited, exhilarated, triumphant heat.

For the first time ever, I'd left Alexi Galanti completely speechless. He didn't have a snarky remark, an amused comeback. He had nothing.

His gaze glided over me in return. And I felt the burn go through me like wildfire.

'So, you're a woman, are you?' I could hear the edge in his voice, but I could also see the arousal—adding a silver glint to the deep blue of his irises—and knew he was testing me. He wanted to scare me off as he had so many times before.

And suddenly I knew why he had treated me like a child long after I had become a woman. Remy was right—he wanted me. But that gallant streak which he had always pretended didn't exist—the gallant streak which made him take his father's fists to protect his brother—had prevented him from taking what he wanted. What we both wanted.

The revelation was like a balm to my soul. And a spur to my senses. It felt how I imagined taking the chequered flag in Bahrain or Melbourne or Barcelona two seconds ahead of the field would feel like. Breathtaking and wonderful, exhilarating and life-affirming all at once.

I'd taken an enormous risk and here was my reward.

'Yes, I'm a woman,' I said, my voice clearer and more certain now. 'And I have been for a while. You've just pretended not to see it.' But he saw it now, I realised, when he put on his jeans in front of me, almost daring me to drink my fill as he tugged them on and buttoned the fly. So of course I did.

He hadn't said anything but, as he turned into the light, I noticed the bruising on his jaw.

'He hit you,' I said, lifting my hand to soothe him.

His arm shot out and he clasped my wrist in an iron grip, preventing my fingers from reaching the skin.

'Don't,' he said. The word was expelled on a tortured rasp and the subtle whiff of tequila on his breath—and my heart silently broke in two at the wary look on his face. 'I don't need your pity,' he said, but I could hear the pain.

It was so real and vivid, it made my stomach ache.

His grip loosened and then he dropped my hand and looked down. The defeated stoop of his shoulders, the exhaustion in his stance, burned away my intense anger at his father until all that was left was the grief. And the longing.

I stepped closer and cradled his cheeks in my hands. He stiffened, but made no move to stop me this time.

I stared into those beautiful blue eyes, for once unguarded, and saw the sadness there, which made me want to weep. But I could also see the desire.

The love I had always had for him—this proud, stubborn, foolishly gallant man—flowed through me and I let every ounce of it shine in my eyes.

'Damn it,' he said as he covered my hands with his but didn't move to pull them away from his jaw. 'Don't look at me like that, *bella notte.*'

The nickname sounded like an endearment as his voice came out on a husky rasp.

'Like what?' I asked.

'Like you want me,' he said. 'Because I'm screwed up enough right now to take you up on the offer and to hell with the consequences.'

Excitement and yearning leapt in my heart and I told him the truth I'd locked inside me for far too long. 'But I *do* want you, Alexi. I always have. And I don't care about the consequences.'

The helicopter touched down on the helipad, jolting me out of my reverie.

Stop it. Stop thinking about that night. About the man you thought you knew.

I rubbed my hands over my face, then gripped my

bag tightly enough to score the leather as the big black machine's blades whirred to a stop.

This trip was going to be hard enough to negotiate without me reliving the painful past. I needed to control the memories and the desire that came with them.

A young man appeared from the back entrance of the house to greet me. I took careful breaths to steady my nerves and the inappropriate heat as he helped me down from the helicopter and took my bag.

'Mademoiselle Simpson, I am Pierre Dupont, Monsieur Galanti's assistant. I hope your journey was good?'

'Yes, very, thanks,' I replied, even though the memory of the journey was a blur now—the chauffeur-driven car to the airport, the flight on Team Galanti's private jet, and the subsequent helicopter ride—my mind still anchored in the past.

I shook my head, trying to jog the memories loose.

'Monsieur Galanti is awaiting your arrival with his legal team,' Pierre said as he ushered me into the house. The familiar smell hit me—a mix of lemon polish, old wood and fresh flowers reminding me, not just of my childhood, but also my mother and her titanic efforts to make the imposing, ornate property a welcoming, homely place despite the anguish that had lurked inside.

I swallowed past the choking sensation in my throat.

Time to get a grip, Belle.

I'd indulged myself enough already. This wasn't the home I'd once known. I was entering enemy territory. And Alexi wasn't my lover any more—if he ever had been—he was my adversary.

Instead of leading me to Gustavo's old office in the east wing of the house, a place where I knew Alexi had often been 'disciplined' by his father as a teenager, Pierre directed me up the stairs to a suite of bright, airy rooms on the first floor. I recognised the door leading to the sunlit terrace immediately, because no one had been allowed to enter this section of the house when I had lived in the villa's grounds as a child.

Because these rooms had belonged to Gustavo's wife, Amelie.

As Pierre opened the door to her former salon, sunshine glinted on the office's modern furniture, but it was the silhouette of the man in the far corner staring through the salon's terrace doors that got all my attention.

Dressed in an expertly tailored business suit which accentuated his tall, lean frame, Alexi had his back to me. He didn't move but tension rippled across his shoulder blades as I was introduced to the four other men in suits who sat in front of his desk.

One of them, a distinguished man in his fifties, offered his hand with a friendly smile. 'Mademoiselle Simpson, I am Etienne Severo, Monsieur Galanti's lead attorney.'

I took his hand and introduced myself, but my gaze remained glued to Alexi as he finally turned.

The sun cast his face into shadow, making it impossible to gauge his reaction. Was he bitter, angry, as wary as I was about this meeting? My heart thudded in my chest, along with the brutal heat that refused to die.

He nodded his own greeting as he walked around his desk. But, as Etienne Severo suggested we sit down so he could outline Monsieur Galanti's plans, Alexi interrupted him.

'So you came?' His voice was flat, but I didn't sense anger in the tone so much as contempt. 'I didn't think you'd have the guts.'

I blinked, taken aback by his hostility even though I had expected it. 'I want to try and make this right and help you form a relationship with your son.'

One sceptical eyebrow rose up Alexi's forehead.

'Do you really?' Disdain and mistrust dripped from his lips. 'And how exactly do you propose to do that when I have missed the formative years of his life through your actions?'

The edge of anger and judgement was rapier-sharp now. So the gloves were already off, if they had ever been on.

I could try to defend my silence or simply ignore the barb—his question after all was a rhetorical one—but this meeting was supposed to be about Cai, not me. And not our previous liaison. So I attempted to answer honestly.

'By...' I swallowed around my dry throat. 'By answering any questions you have about him. And letting you know what an incredible child he is.'

'So you've told him about me?' he asked, but it

was another cynical question, his voice tense with suspicion, the anger sparkling in his eyes.

I didn't dislodge my gaze, even though I wanted to.

'I've talked in generalities with him about you. He's never asked about his father, but he's curious now, and I think he'll be ready to meet you soon.' It had only been a week since our chance encounter, but I'd already begun to prepare the ground for Cai to meet Alexi. I wanted my son to be excited about meeting his father, but I also wanted to be sure Alexi wouldn't take his anger with me out on our son.

'*How* soon?'

'I don't know, when did you have in mind?' I asked, struggling to be civil in the face of his enmity. He was baiting me. This wasn't about Cai—this was about his anger with me.

'How about I have him flown out here tomorrow?' he asked, stepping closer, his big body rippling with barely concealed rage.

'No!' I said, forcing myself to stand my ground.

'No?' he said, his voice rising. 'What gives you the right to keep my son from me a moment longer?'

'Because I'm his mother.'

'And I'm his father. A fact you chose to forget for five years.'

'You're also a stranger to him,' I pointed out.

'And who's fault is that?' he shouted, the anger unleashed.

'It's my fault,' I admitted. 'Mostly.'

I wasn't the only one to blame—maybe if he hadn't rejected me so thoroughly all those years ago, maybe if he hadn't destroyed my confidence and my self-worth, I might not have been scared to contact him. Scared he would reject Cai the way he had rejected me.

'Mostly?' The word sliced into me, harsh and unyielding.

But before I could defend myself Severo cleared his throat loudly. 'Perhaps we could sit down and outline your offer to Mademoiselle Simpson, Alexi?'

Alexi stared at him blankly for a moment, and I wondered if he had forgotten the legal team was in the room.

'Actually, I wish to speak with Mademoiselle Simpson in private.'

The other men nodded and started to gather the papers strewn across Alexi's desk, probably more than happy to leave us to it, but before any of them could leave Severo surprised me.

'Is this acceptable to you, Mademoiselle Simpson?' he asked. I had to give him credit for standing up to Alexi, his employer, on my behalf, especially as he had to sense the animosity between us.

Heat fired across my collarbone as Alexi waited for my answer, challenge as well as contempt in his expression. He was expecting me to refuse, possibly to run away again. The way I had five years ago.

And I couldn't deny the urge to do so.

Being alone in a room with him felt perilous for a number of reasons, but I knew I wasn't scared of him, or his anger. Not any more. I wasn't the naïve, easily bruised nineteen-year-old he'd rejected so cruelly five years ago, and he wasn't the grief-stricken man torn apart by guilt for his brother's death. He was the father of my child. And that meant we had to find a way through this. Somehow.

So I nodded. 'Yes, I'll talk with Monsieur Galanti alone.'

Severo nodded back before he and the other lawyers left.

'Sit down,' Alexi said, indicating a large leather arm chair as he strode across the carpet to sit behind his desk. I wondered if he needed to create distance between us as much as I did. Were the memories of our one night together as hard for him to ignore as they were for me?

Whatever his motives, the endorphins making every one of my pulse points pound relaxed as he stepped away from me.

He propped his elbows on the desk, those pure blue eyes skewering me to the spot as he studied me.

I waited for him to speak first.

'Why?' he asked at last. 'Why didn't you tell me about the boy's existence?' The words were clipped, his frustration clear, but unfortunately I didn't have a straight answer for him.

'I'm sorry,' I apologised again. 'I should have contacted you a long—'

'I don't want an apology.' He cut in. 'I want to know why. Is it because you weren't sure if I was the father?'

The hurt at his mistrust of me was like a blow. So we were back to that again. I hated that he was forc-

ing me to admit again how vulnerable I had been that
night, but I refused to be defensive.

'I told you, you were my first lover,' I replied.

'So you say, but you didn't behave like a virgin.
You were so…' His gaze seared my skin, the memories pounding back to life.

'I was so what?' I said. 'So un-virgin-like?'

'So responsive, so eager.' He growled the words
as if they were an insult. But my stupid body didn't
take the comment as an insult. Instead the husky rasp
made the fire inside me spark and spit.

'How many women have an orgasm their first
time?' he added. 'Unless you faked that too?'

I leapt out of the chair. 'You bastard. I didn't fake
anything. I enjoyed it. I wanted it. I wanted you. I'd
wanted to find out what all the fuss about sex was
for a long time,' I added quickly, in case he read too
much into that bald statement. The truth was I hadn't
wanted sex with anyone. I'd wanted Alexi to be my
first, had dreamed about what it would be like, and
he had not disappointed me. I hadn't just had one orgasm, I'd had several. But I'd be damned if I'd compliment him on his performance when he was already
holding my response against me.

'If I was really your first, why didn't you tell me
that?' he countered and I wanted to scream. 'Don't
all women want their first lover to know?'

'Of course not,' I shot back. 'You've obviously
never been a nineteen-year-old girl. The *last* thing I
wanted was for you to know I'd never done it before.'
Duh. 'You were gorgeous and sophisticated and six

years older than me. I'd had a massive crush on you for as long as I could remember. I wanted you to see me as a woman. Not a little girl.'

'You didn't bleed,' he said, still interrogating me.

The anger I'd carefully held at bay ripped through me to join the riot of inappropriate hormonal responses.

'So what? I don't have to prove my virginity to you. I don't actually care whether you believe I was a virgin or not. I only told you because I wanted you to know how I knew Cai was your son.'

We were talking in circles, I realised. Pointless circles. I already knew I would never be able to break through the wall of cynicism that made him believe every woman was a cheat, an actress, a liar. And I had not come here to try.

'But what about Remy?' he said. 'You expect me to believe you didn't sleep with him when he loved you and you say you loved him?'

'It was never like that between us—we were just friends.' I wanted to say we'd been like brother and sister, but that would have been doing a disservice to our friendship. Remy and I had never fought, never argued. Unlike siblings, there had been no rivalry between us, only support and love. We had always had each other's backs, had always been there for each other. God, I wished he was here for me right now, so he could knock some sense into his brother.

'Don't make me laugh. No man would be able to love you like he did and not want to take that *friend-*

ship…' he made sarcastic air quotes, making the anger thrum in my chest '…to its logical conclusion.'

'Unless he was a gay man,' I said.

'What?' he croaked.

Guilt ripped into me and I sat down again. I hadn't intended to tell him about Remy so cold-bloodedly… I hadn't even really considered telling him at all. Why would I reveal Remy's secret now when I had respected my friend's privacy for so long? But I hadn't expected to be subjected to an inquisition about my virginity.

Why was Alexi so hung up about that detail of our liaison?

'I'm sorry,' I said grudgingly but, as I watched the truth he had never acknowledged about his brother cross his face, the guilt blossomed under my breastbone.

I had always known this would be hard for Alexi— finding out his brother had never confided in him, discovering that their relationship had not been as close as he'd thought—but I couldn't hold on to the lies a moment longer.

'Remy was gay,' I reiterated, the anger fading and leaving me shaky and sad. 'He had his first boyfriend when he was fourteen. He never wanted me in that way because he didn't desire women.'

I sunk into the chair, suddenly exhausted. I'd got up at four that morning, left my child sleeping and been on a knife-edge of stress for days, but that wasn't what was making my bones feel so weary. It was the renewed flicker of compassion as I watched the bone-deep regret cross Alexi's face.

'But if that's true, why didn't he tell me?' he whispered. 'Did he think I would reject him? That I would love him any less? That I was some kind of narrow-minded bigot?'

I hadn't wanted to reopen this raw wound. Alexi was probably still beating himself up about Remy's death, because that was the kind of man he was, jealously guarding his pain so he didn't have to share it with anyone, or show any weakness.

'No, of course not,' I said. 'Remy *knew* you loved him, because he knew all about the abuse you took from Gustavo to protect him.'

Alexi's gaze hardened, as I knew it would. This was his private pain too. Stuff I was supposed to pretend didn't matter, hadn't affected him. But it was this secrecy which had made it impossible for Remy to confide in his brother. That needed to end now.

'What are you talking about?' he said.

'*We* knew,' I said. 'About the extent of the abuse, Alexi. The back-handed slaps, the casual violence. We could hear the shouting, the things he said to you late at night when you both thought we were in bed. We saw the bruises, the split lips, the black eyes you pretended were caused by anything else but him. Remy knew how homophobic your father was. He kept his sexuality a secret because he thought he had to, to protect you from having to protect him from your father's abuse. Again. That night…'

My breathing became ragged, the memories flowing back, the emotion, the pain, as real as the desire. 'I came to you because I'd overheard your father shouting at you again. He hit you. And you didn't hit him back, even though you could have. You were bigger and stronger than him, but you took it, the way you always did. I could see how angry you were, how humiliated, and I wanted to help, to make it better somehow.'

'What are you saying?' he demanded as he strode round the desk. 'That the night we made our son was a pity screw? That you sacrificed your virginity to make me feel better about the fact my father hated my guts?'

I stood up and tilted my head so I could look into his eyes, brutally aware of the unyielding strength of his body, the tension vibrating through him and the pulse of desire making my knees dissolve. I shook my head because I had never pitied him, only loved him.

Going with instinct, I touched his cheek. I wasn't infatuated with him any more, I could see all his weaknesses now, but a part of me still ached for that valiant young man who had always protected his brother.

The bunched muscle in his jaw clenched against my palm as he jerked his head free.

I dropped my hand. I should not have touched him. But, as I stared into his eyes, all I could see was the same rage and pain I'd wanted to soothe that night.

I didn't want to soothe it any more. Because I knew I couldn't.

'Don't touch me, Belle, or you'll be sorry again,' he said.

'I'm not sorry,' I said, the foolish urge to take away his pain getting the better of me. 'I've never been sorry. I got Cai out of it, and the best sex of my life.'

The *only* sex of my life.

He swore viciously, but then his own hands cradled my cheeks. 'Why do you tempt me still?'

I wasn't sure if it was a question meant for me or himself, but I answered it anyway. 'I can't help it,' I whispered.

His fingers threaded into my hair, sending flying the pins that I'd used to tame the red mass.

'Tell me to stop,' he said, his voice tortured as he tilted my head back.

'I can't.' I shuddered, giving him the tacit permission he sought.

The wave of need slammed into me as his lips fastened on my neck, his teeth and tongue feasting on my throat as he sucked on the pulse point. I shivered as his erection pressed into my belly and my fingers gripped his shirt to drag him closer.

His arms banded around my waist at last, his fingers roaming freely under my blouse. Pleasure blossomed inside me, tightening my nipples.

At last his mouth found mine, his tongue plunging deep—tempting, taking, conquering.

I met his demands with demands of my own. It had been so long since I'd felt this need, this desire, so long since I'd been wanted in this way. But, just as my senses surrendered to everything I knew he could do for me, a loud knock sounded at the door.

We jumped apart so fast, it was as if a water cannon had been fired at us.

Alexi rubbed his chin, swearing softly as he stared at me as if I'd grown an extra head, while I struggled to get my breathing under some semblance of control.

It would almost have been funny, like the scene from a bad sitcom, if the implications of what we'd just done….or rather, had *almost* done…weren't so catastrophic.

What exactly had I been thinking? I'd pretty much jumped him. I was a grown woman, and a mother. I should have been able to resist the desire that had flared like a firecracker as soon as I touched him.

Alexi was still my kryptonite—that much was obvious.

But I'd paid dearly once before for letting my desire rule my head. And for thinking that sex, especially the stupendous, incendiary sex that was clearly still our MO, was a substitute for emotional engagement.

I'd been emotionally engaged when I'd made love to him the first time. And he had not been. I wouldn't get sucked into that vortex again.

'Monsieur Galanti, there is an urgent call for you from the Paris office, and Monsieur Severo would like to know if you wish to delay the negotiations with Mademoiselle Simpson until tomorrow morning.' I recognised the voice of his assistant and realised for the first time that the sun was beginning its descent in the distance. It had to be after six o'clock. Obviously Monsieur Severo and his team were keen to get the business portion of the day over with.

'I'll take the call from Paris, and tell Etienne Mademoiselle Simpson will be with them shortly,' Alexi rasped, dragging his fingers through his hair as he continued to stare at me, probably struggling to make sense of what had *almost* happened just now as much as I was.

'I should leave,' I said, the panic starting to overwhelm me. Staying the night on this estate with this man, and all the memories, was fraught with danger. I'd thought I could hack it. I was a lot less sure now. But, as I went to pick up my bag, Alexi touched my wrist.

'Don't…' He ran his fingertip up my arm. Could he feel my instinctive shudder? Probably… But I was way past being humiliated by my response to him. 'Don't go, I want you to stay.'

'Why?' I asked.

Desire blazed in his eyes for a moment and I was almost scalded by the intensity of it. But then he lifted his fingertip from my arm and tucked his hand into his trouser pocket. 'Because there is much for my legal team to discuss with you…about our son. I have four years of back maintenance to pay, to begin with.'

I stiffened. 'Is that why you brought me here, to offer me money? I don't want your money.'

Did he still think I was a gold-digger?

'I know that,' he countered, and the clutching sensation in my stomach released. At least I wasn't still beating my head against that brick wall any more. 'But that doesn't alter the fact I owe you money,' he added. 'You and my son. I know it hasn't been easy for you both since you left Monaco. That you have student loans, a mortgage and other debts. I wish to set up a trust fund for the boy, and give you a generous allowance for his care that will be backdated.'

How did he know so much about my finances? But as soon as I'd asked the question I could guess the answer. He would have had me investigated. I'd expected as much.

But I didn't want his money. It would compromise me. I didn't want to give him any ownership of my life, and that included allowing him to pay my debts or give me maintenance. But I forced myself not to reject the suggestion out of hand.

A trust fund for Cai, I could accept. But before I did that we needed to talk about our son. That was why I was really here. And that was what I should concentrate on now. Not the heat between us that would not die.

'Your son has a name,' I said quietly.

He frowned. And I realised we had a very long way to go before I could introduce him to Cai. Was he even curious about his son? He hadn't really asked me anything personal about him yet, hadn't once referred to him by name. Jessie had been right—this was a relationship for which he wasn't remotely prepared.

'You're right, I know nothing about Cai,' he said, the deliberateness with which he made himself say his son's name making me want to weep. 'If you stay, we can work out the financial arrangements and also have a chance to talk about him. I have missed all his formative years,' he went on and, while the edge of accusation was no longer there, I could still hear it in my head.

I was the one who had denied them both that emotional connection with my silence. Whether or not Alexi was capable of being a father, how much he even wanted to be one, remained to be seen. But it was no longer for me to make those decisions for him or Cai. 'I never expected to become a father, so this is new territory for me,' he added. 'And I accept that where the boy is concerned I will need your guidance—which is precisely why I'm asking you to stay...' He paused, his stance stiff, uncomfortable and oddly defensive for a man who rarely, if ever, admitted a weakness. 'I'm not sure how much of a father I can be to him.'

He shoved both his hands into the pockets of his suit trousers.

I had the weirdest feeling he was trying to prevent himself from touching me. The thought was disturbing on one level, but oddly comforting on another. At least I wasn't the only one struggling here.

'So what is your answer?' he asked. 'Will you stay so we can continue to discuss this?'

I looked past him, out into the villa's grounds, the landscaped gardens, the pool, the beach. However hard this was for me, it was time I faced my past—and started preparing myself and my son for our future. A future with Alexi Galanti in it. And learning to rationalise and control my body's response to him was as much a part of that as anything else.

Turning back to him, I nodded. 'Okay, I'll stay.'

My stomach chose that precise moment to rumble louder than the helicopter in which I had arrived. Not all that surprising, given that I hadn't eaten today, the nerves having got the better of me on the flight over, but still mortifying.

Alexi let out a strained laugh as he watched my face ignite. 'I will arrange for some supper to be served while you meet with my legal team.'

'You're not joining us?' I asked, then wished I could pull the question back. Why had my voice sounded so eager?

'Etienne has my authority to outline my wishes. If there is anything you are not happy with, we can discuss it tomorrow.'

I nodded. 'That makes sense,' I said, trying to sound pleased and not stupidly bereft at the thought of not seeing him until tomorrow.

What was wrong with me? Speaking to Etienne and his team without Alexi there would make it much easier not to let the knot of emotion in my stomach override my reason again.

But, just as I was congratulating myself on my pragmatism, he took his hand out of his pocket and tucked a tendril of hair behind my ear.

The sizzle of reaction shot through me, as shocking as it was debilitating.

'I will see you tomorrow, *bella notte*,' he murmured, his voice as husky as my wayward thoughts. 'Sweet dreams.'

As he walked away, the yearning surged and I knew this relationship was going to be much tougher to negotiate than I had ever thought possible.

I might have grown up in the last five years, but unfortunately I hadn't grown immune to Alexi Galanti. Not even close.

And now he knew it.

CHAPTER FIVE

Alexi

As I stood on the balcony of my suite of rooms, I imagined Belle in the cottage where I had insisted she be accommodated after the combustible moment we'd shared before her meeting with Etienne and his team.

The guest house on the edge of the property was as far away from me as it was possible to put her. But, as I gazed down onto the pool terrace below my balcony, the site of our torrid liaison all those years ago, the night we'd made our son, I knew geographical distance was not going to control the yearning still pounding through my system.

What an arrogant fool I'd been to think she had no hold on me any more. How could I have kidded myself that my demand to bring her here—a place where I'd rarely stayed since my brother's death—was all about the boy? A clever tactic to unsettle her which would help me get the upper hand in any negotiations…

Yes, it had unsettled her. But it had also unsettled me.

So much for having control of this damn situation. I felt less in control now than I had when I'd met her again a week ago and discovered I had a son. The night was warm, but not as warm as my skin, or the pulsing ache in my groin which had refused to subside ever since our kiss in my office four hours ago.

Kiss—who was I kidding? That hadn't been a kiss, it had been an explosion of need, desire and something else. Something I definitely did not want to name, let alone think about. But how could I not, when my balcony gave me an uninterrupted view of the pool—the place where I had lost myself once before?

I wet my dry throat with a sip of the vintage Cognac I usually kept for special occasions. The liquor burned my throat as I swallowed. My skin felt tight and hot, my heart beating an erratic rhythm.

When I'd received the results of the DNA test and discovered that the boy was mine, that Remy was not the father, my feelings had been mixed. First shock, then anger that I had been denied this knowledge for so long, but underneath it all had been a strange sense of joy which I could no more explain than my incendiary reaction to Belle's touch this afternoon.

I was not parent material, had never even considered becoming a father. But my feelings towards the boy, towards becoming a father so unexpectedly, were nowhere near as volatile as my feelings for his mother.

Especially as I now knew the truth, not just about her virginity, but about Remy.

Had I always known my brother was gay? I think I had. It sickened me to realise all the signs had been there. I had spent the last few hours—ever since Belle's revelation—recalling the conversations I'd had with Remy about dating in the last few years of his life. The enquiries he'd avoided answering, the jokes he'd laughed at with a strained smile—even our final conversation when Remy had seemed so pleased about my one-night stand with his best friend which I had been determined to believe was a cover for some secret heartbreak.

Remy had been showing me the truth all along and I had failed to see it.

Was that the real reason I had been torn apart by guilt after his death—because I'd tried to blame Belle when the only person who had really betrayed Remy was me? Not by sleeping with his girl, but by refusing to see him as he really was. By avoiding that truth because it had been easier than having to deal with it—having to support him and defend him against our father's prejudices.

Maybe Belle had been a coward not to tell me about my son. But I had been an even bigger coward, not supporting Remy, not ensuring he knew he could be honest with me.

I stared down at the pool, the lights giving the water a bright-blue glow, and the knots in my stomach released. I could almost hear Remy's voice—

laughing, cheeky, kind and optimistic—telling me to let go of the guilt.

Belle was right. What the hell was the point of feeling guilty now about how I had let my brother down? I couldn't go back and fix the mistakes I'd made.

We knew.

My stomach tensed again. I slugged back the rest of the Cognac.

I was not going there, or I'd only feel more confused. More angry. More humiliated. I'd kidded myself that I was protecting my brother when all the time he—and Belle, with her silence about his sexuality—had been protecting me.

I reached for the bottle to refill my glass. But then my hand paused.

Not the answer, Alexi.

Alcohol was never the answer. I, of all people, ought to know that.

I slammed down the glass and glanced back at the pool. I'd gone down there that night to cool off because I'd been so mad at my father for turning to drink, first and foremost, and at my mother for abandoning Remy and me all those years ago. But right now a cold swim felt like a better solution than sulking in my room and getting drunk.

The memories were going to haunt me anyway—there was no avoiding them. Heading down to the pool now and diving into that frigid water wasn't going to make them any worse. And it might finally kill the heat that had been messing with my head ever since I'd turned and spotted Belle standing in my mother's old parlour this afternoon—her eyes wary, intelligent and guarded.

I'd brought her here to pay her off. To pay off my responsibilities to the child, to manage the fall-out from that night long ago. I'd wanted to be angry with her for her deception, wanted to believe she was guilty of everything I'd ever accused her of in my grief, guilt and loneliness, even though I'd already known before she'd arrived most of it wasn't true.

I had read the report from the private investigator whom Etienne had hired on my behalf. I knew exactly how hard it had been for her financially, especially during the early years of our son's life—after I had banished her and threatened her with arrest. I had been wrong, not just about her relationship with my brother, but about my desire for her. I had always tried to pretend it was nothing more than a one-night stand brought about by alcohol, loneliness and opportunity.

The minute she had touched my face, though, the minute she had looked into my eyes, I had seen her compassion, but also her desire, and my body's re-sponse had made me acknowledge how much I had lied to myself.

But I wasn't the only one lying.

I still wanted her—as much as, if not more than, I had five years ago—but she still wanted me. And now I needed to decide what I was going to do about that too.

Etienne had told me an hour ago Belle had refused the financial package I was offering her. But I was determined my son—and by extension his mother—would be financially secure.

Marching out of my bedroom suite, I headed down the stairs and walked out into the night. It was warm for May, the sultry breeze filling with the scent of wildflowers. But, as I crossed the villa's *terrazzo* and took the steps winding down to the pool, the memories blindsided me again. I felt tense and edgy, my skin prickling with the unrequited desire I couldn't seem to tame, but instead of struggling to hold the memories in, as I stripped off my clothes and dived into the pool, I let them flood through me again as I sunk beneath the crisp, cool water.

'But I do want you, Alexi. I always have. And I don't care about the consequences.'

As I stood on the pool terrace, my mind tried to engage with what Belle was saying to me.

Who was this girl? Because it wasn't the tomboy whose thick braids made her hair look like a couple of hunks of vibrant red rope, the kid who had trailed around after my brother, Remy, for years and got into no end of trouble with him.

I couldn't ignore the evidence of my eyes any longer. She wore the same shimmering green dress she'd worn a month ago to the Galanti summer ball. I hadn't recognised her at first that night, and after I had I'd tried to ignore her. But I'd known then I was already in big trouble. Because she didn't look like a kid any more. She looked like a woman. A beautiful woman.

And tonight she didn't just look like a beauti-

ful woman, she looked like a goddess, wild and un-
tamed. Her vibrant red hair—no longer pinned up
in a sophisticated concoction of curls, as it had been
at the ball—caught the moonlight, creating a fiery
halo around her head. Those slanting eyes were the
colour of rough-cut emeralds, and her high breasts
pressed against the tight bodice. Barefoot, brave and
unashamed, she was like some Greek water nymph—
beautiful, bold and devastating to my peace of mind.

Heat throbbed and surged in my groin, stiffen-
ing my shaft and making me forget about the ache
in my jaw where my father had lashed out to end our
argument.

With Belle I had always felt like a person instead
of a shadow. But I felt like much more than just a
person now. The sweet passion and approval in those
emerald pools weren't just soothing all the feelings of
inadequacy which had haunted me since childhood.
They were firing my soul.

What was so wrong with wanting her for myself,
just this once?

Tonight I needed her so I could feel like part of
the world. To take away the hollow ache in my soul
that had always been there. Ever since the night my
mother had left and my father had used his fists on
me for the first time.

I didn't want to think about consequences, about
the past or the future. I just wanted to live in the now.

Reaching out of their own accord, my palms caressed the shimmering silk.

Her breath gushed out against my lips, her arms reaching around me as her body bowed to mine.

I tasted her for the first time. She was like nectar— both sweet and spicy, both refreshing and addictive. I knew I should take things slowly. Be careful with her, be kind. How much experience did she have? But then her fingers curled into my hair, her nails scraping across my scalp, and sensation arrowed into my sex, turning my erection to iron.

Her tongue tangled with mine in fast, furious strokes as if she couldn't get enough of my taste. I knew how she felt. The hunger was consuming me as I dragged her against the thick ridge in my pants and ground it against her soft curves so she would know how much I needed her.

She didn't flinch or squeal, she matched my hunger with hunger of her own. My mind, or what was left of it, rejoiced. This was not a woman without experience, or how could she know exactly how to touch and taste me to drive me insane?

The last of my inhibitions died as I scooped her into my arms and carried her to a lounger. She lay panting, her eyes wild, her full breasts heaving against the floaty material. Material I'd wanted to rip off her the first time I'd seen her in the damn thing.

Her hair lay around her and I imagined that mermaid in the cartoon she used to love watching when she'd first come to live with us.

The thought should have had a sobering effect. But remembering her as a kid only seemed to make me more aware of how much older she was now.

Not a girl, a woman. A seductress in full charge of her sexuality.

I wanted to tear the sheer fabric, but forced myself to control the urge.

'I want you so damn much,' I admitted.

Her skin flushed, the sight breathtaking as her lips spread into a smile that consumed her whole face and left me feeling a little dazed, a lot dazzled.

'Me too,' she said on a breathless whisper so full of longing, I was surprised my head didn't explode.

I lay down beside her, forced myself to go slow. She might know what she did to me, but that didn't mean I didn't want to cherish this moment. I couldn't offer her permanence. This would be a one-time deal. But it would be the best deal she'd ever had.

I brushed my thumb over the rigid nipple visible through her dress. The violent shiver which racked her body at the light caress made me chuckle.

'*Dio*, when did you grow into such a beautiful woman?' I said, because it still puzzled me. One minute she had been tagging around with my kid brother, climbing trees, causing trouble, and then a month ago everything had changed. She'd walked into the summer ball on Remy's arm, her curves spotlighted by the dress, her eyes connecting with mine, and all I'd wanted to do was ditch the woman on my own arm and fall to my knees in front of her.

Remy had been teasing me about my reaction ever since.

'Years ago,' she whispered.

'What about Remy?' I asked as I trailed my thumb

over the pulse point in her neck—but the truth was I was finding it hard to care about my brother's claim on her. If Remy cared about her, why wasn't he here instead of heading out for the evening in Nice with a group of his friends? 'I thought you were his girl.'

She blinked and something crossed her face, but then she said, 'I'm nobody's girl. I'm a woman, and I make my own decisions.'

Blood pounded in my groin and I gave up trying to think coherently as I scooped a handful of her hair into my fist and tugged her lips back to mine. I'd always tried to protect Remy, not just from our father's anger but also our mother's neglect. But I wanted to take this one thing for myself. How could it be wrong when I needed her so much? Remy had always joked about their relationship, never staked a claim to her. Why should I care, if he didn't?

I sunk into the fragrant mass, which smelled of flowers and sea, as my mouth captured hers. She bowed back, her breasts rubbing against my chest like a cat desperate to be stroked.

I cupped the warm flesh, slipped my hand beneath the bodice. My hunger roared as I found naked flesh and her nipple swelled against my palm.

Dio! She wasn't wearing a bra.

All the fantasies I'd had about her in the last month, fantasies I had tried so hard to tame, flooded through my brain and had every last molecule of reason plummeting into my pants.

Her palm cradled me, gauging the size and weight of my erection.

I jolted. Her touch was like lightning. My palm glided up her thigh under the floaty fabric to trace the sensitive seam of flesh at the top of her leg. She shuddered and moaned, the raw thirst like a flare to my libido.

I pressed the heel of my hand against her vulva, felt the damp heat of her panties then slipped my finger inside the gusset to find the plump lips of her sex swollen and ready for me.

Grasping handfuls of the dress, I tugged it up.

'Sit up,' I ordered, and she obeyed, allowing me to drag the garment over her head. I threw it away then helped her to wriggle out of her panties.

Her naked body glowed in the moonlight, the sprinkle of freckles across her collarbone like a trail of stars leading me home.

I captured the stiff peak between hungry lips. I flicked and nuzzled the pebbled tip until she was panting with need, while my fingers explored the slick seam of her sex and found the swollen nub.

As if she had been primed and ready for me, she choked off a sob.

'Come for me, *bella notte*,' I demanded, frantic to see her shatter.

Her cry echoed in the night and drifted away on the sea breeze. Ecstasy surged through me. I wasn't a shadow, I was a man. I wasn't a nobody, I was somebody. At least, to Belle—whatever my father shouted at me.

Her emerald eyes stared at me, unfocused and dazed, her sweet skin flushed a beautiful pink.

Suddenly I was frantically releasing myself from my trousers, positioning her hips. I couldn't wait any longer. I had no protection with me. I'd never taken a woman without protection in my life, but I promised myself I would pull out before it was too late.

She wrapped her fingers around my shaft, her thumb trailing across the head, and I had to bite off a sob of my own. But I forced myself to slow down, to ask, 'Are you sure?'

'Yes,' she said, her confidence and certainty humbling me.

Notching my erection to her entrance, I pressed in slowly. I forced myself not to thrust too hard. She was tight, incredibly tight, but she didn't flinch or turn away. She lifted her hips and wrapped her legs around my waist. Welcoming me home as she clung to me, her nails dug into my shoulders, only increasing the sensory overload.

At last I was lodged deep. Our ragged breathing sounded loud in the quiet night. I felt conquered and all-conquering.

'Are you okay?' I asked. Had I ever felt this incredible inside a woman before? I didn't think so. 'You're very tight.'

She nodded. 'It feels wonderful.' She sighed. I shifted and her voice broke on a raw gasp. I had found her G-spot.

I rocked my hips, out and back, digging into that tender spot—euphoria licking at my spine and turning my limbs to jelly as she reacted like a wild thing.

I wanted to last, wanted to make this as magnificent for her as it was for me, but I could feel the orgasm crashing towards me. I held on, held back, kept pushing, kept thrusting, kept digging. Each sweet sigh, each staggered sob, added to the frenzy working through me.

At last her muscles clamped around me, massaging my length, and my climax roared through me.

I collapsed on top of her, hollowed out, spent, but as soon as the afterglow began to fade and my breathing evened out I knew I'd made a terrible mistake.

I saw Remy's face—open, joking, laughing, uncomplicated and so loyal—and disgust ripped through me. The shadows returned in a rush, chilling my body as I withdrew and felt her flinch.

Doing up my trousers, I got off the lounger and passed her the dress.

'Is everything okay, Alexi?' she asked, suddenly sounding like a little girl again, wary and unsure.

'I didn't use a condom,' I said, turning my back so she could get dressed.

I dragged unsteady fingers through my hair, appalled at my actions.

'I… I'm sorry… I think it's okay, though. I've only just finished my period.' Her voice sounded small, hesitant, embarrassed. And the shame engulfed me.

'Don't be sorry,' I said. 'Just let me know if there's a problem.'

I turned back. Thank God she had donned the dress and her panties. But she still looked… Heat pulsed. I needed to leave, to get out of here, before I took her again.

'Okay?' I said, more sharply than I had intended.

She nodded, her eyes wide. 'Yes, Alexi.'

'Are you going to the track tomorrow?' I asked, sickened with myself when she nodded.

Of course she would be there, to see Remy test the new car. He would want her there because she was his girl, not mine.

'Don't tell Remy what happened between us. It was a mistake, okay?' I said.

She looked down, her fingers clutched together, the knuckles white. Her shoulders trembled imperceptibly and I felt like a bastard. The bastard my father had always accused me of being. Was she going to cry? Damn it.

Capturing her chin, I lifted her face to mine.

'Do you understand, Belle? It was a mistake. It's not going to happen again, we're not dating,' I said, keeping my voice cool even though the heat was still thrumming through my system like a ballistic missile.

She nodded again.

'Say it,' I demanded.

'I understand, Alexi. We're not dating. It was a mistake.'

I wanted to kiss her, to apologise—she looked so forlorn—but I resisted the urge and let go of her chin. Those deep pools of green were filled with sadness, but I forced the prickle of anger to the fore. I wasn't the only one who had cheated on my brother. She had cheated on him too.

I surged out of the water, the memories of that night five years ago so strong and vivid still, I almost expected to see Belle hiding beside the pool house all over again in that devastating green dress. But tonight the pool terrace was empty, the lights from Monte Carlo blinking in the distance as I climbed out and stood on the stones. I shuddered as I grabbed a towel, but the salt-scented breeze didn't do enough to cool the heat still rioting through my body, or banish the regret.

I'd been a selfish bastard that night. She *had* been a virgin—it had been so obvious but I'd ignored all the evidence to absolve my own guilt. And she was right. What had come the day after, the devastating blow of Remy's death, had been nothing more than a tragic accident.

I'd turned on her in my grief, accused and threatened her and sent her away—not just because I felt guilty about what we'd done, devastated by Remy's death, but because I still wanted her too much. And as a result she'd been too scared to tell me I was a father. A part of me was still angry that, but for our chance meeting in Barcelona a week ago, I might never have discovered I had a son but much of that anger was now directed at myself.

According to the feedback I'd got from Etienne about her meeting with the legal team after I'd left them, she was not keen to accept any money from me for herself. And I considered that a problem. I didn't just owe my son. I also owed her.

I dried myself, took off my wet shorts and tugged back on the rest of my clothing. After dumping the towel in the bin by the pool house, I picked up my shoes.

As I walked back through the gardens towards the house in the moonlight, my bare feet warmed by the sun-heated stone, a plan formed.

I wanted Belle to accept my support. But I knew how stubborn she was and how independent.

That said, I also still needed a reserve driver, and her credentials as a fuel-efficiency expert were exemplary. Galanti's latest prototype was still in development and the R&D team was struggling to recruit engineers of her calibre.

Perhaps there was a way to satisfy both my personal responsibilities and my professional needs where Belle was concerned. But I could not risk getting close to her again until I could control the hunger.

As I walked through the silent house to my bedroom, and shucked my damp clothes to step into the shower, the heat that had pounded in my veins ever since that afternoon swelled and throbbed again…

I took the stubborn erection in hand, feeling like a teenage boy. Why could I not control this need?

I pumped my shaft in fast, efficient strokes, the steaming water cascading over my back. The orgasm ripped through me and I let out a muffled shout.

But as I stepped out of the shower and my heartbeat slowed I could feel the tension tightening the muscles at the base of my spine all over again as I imagined seeing Belle again tomorrow—and the heated negotiations that were likely to ensue.

Belle as a love-struck girl was a temptation I had been unable to ignore. Unfortunately, Belle as an independent woman was even more irresistible.

CHAPTER SIX

Belle

'You can't be serious? I can't possibly accept.' I stared at Alexi, concerned not just by the stubborn line of his lips but the traitorous leap in my heart.

Apparently I still yearned for his approval, despite everything that had happened in the last five years. But, what was even more disappointing, I was fairly sure it wasn't just his approval I wanted. I'd spent all night unable to sleep in the luxury surroundings of the guest cottage, obsessing about our kiss.

'Why not? I need a reserve driver and you would be an excellent addition to my development team.'

'It's too much money,' I said. The sum he'd offered to pay me for my work was ridiculous—and I suspected had more to do with what he perceived to be his financial responsibilities to Cai than to me. I had already refused a similar financial settlement offer the day before.

'Of course it's not. Your expertise is unique—the

only reason you believe it is too much is because that cheapskate Camaro is paying you too little.'

'I can't be a reserve driver—I've already told you that.'

'I know you have, but you never gave me an answer as to why not. And don't lie to me and tell me your dreams have changed. No one changes that much. Being a driver was as much your dream as Remy's.'

'Which is precisely why it's not my dream any more,' I said, forcing myself not to flinch at the probing intensity in that pure blue gaze. 'Remy died pursuing his dream. I can't afford to take that risk.'

'The risk is minimal and you know it,' he shot back. 'Remy was never as talented as you are. He was too easily distracted, too confident and too addicted to the adrenaline rush of speed. If he had lived he would have learned to curtail those impulses, but you already have.'

The thrumming in my chest increased, my ribs tightening as the desire to defend Remy's impulsive behaviour was combined with the realisation that I had won Alexi's admiration at last, and it mattered, even though it shouldn't.

'I appreciate the compliment, Alexi, but I don't want to drive professionally any more because I have a son.'

He blinked, clearly surprised by this line of argument, which had my ribs squeezing my lungs. He really was clueless about the responsibilities of parenthood.

'Childcare will not be a problem. Anything you need will be made available,' he said, still not getting it. 'In fact, if you would just accept the financial package my legal team outlined yesterday you wouldn't even need to consider the boy's care a problem.'

'I don't consider Cai's care a problem. But it's not childcare that's the issue.'

'Then what is the issue?' he demanded as he paced towards me, throwing up his arms in exasperation.

'The issue is, I can't and won't risk my life to pursue a dream, however slight the risk, because that would mean leaving my child without the only parent he has.'

He stiffened as if I had slapped him. And I realised what I'd said. Cai didn't have just one parent, he had two. But I held back the knee-jerk apology.

I still wasn't prepared to drive professionally— Alexi was a total stranger to Cai and, even if he weren't, I would never want to leave my child without a mother.

Alexi thrust his fingers through his hair and let out a deep sigh.

'You're right. I had not considered that. And I should have,' he added. 'I'll find someone else for the reserve driver position.'

I stood and placed my fingers on his arm. 'It's okay, Alexi. This is all new to you, I get that,' I said, trying to soothe the flicker of guilt.

His forearm tensed and something else, something hot and volatile, danced in his eyes.

I dropped my hand and tucked it into my pocket. Touching Alexi was not a good idea.

'It'll take a while for you to put Cai's interests first. It's an adjustment we all have to make when we become parents—and you've only effectively been a parent for a week.'

He nodded. His gaze still seared me. 'This is true, but that's not why I should have realised the implications of your decision.'

'I don't… I don't understand,' I said hesitantly, because he'd lost me, and the strange feeling of connection was only intensifying between us.

'I know what it is to be without a mother. I should not wish that on any child. And especially not my own.'

The brutal pain in his eyes shocked me, before he had a chance to mask it, but not as much as the admission of vulnerability. When had Alexi ever been willing to share his pain with me? With anyone?

'I still want you on my R&D team,' he insisted. 'The money is unchanged.'

'I can't… I'm under contract to Renzo. He's been good to me, and Cai, and he's a friend so I can't just…'

'Stop.' He pressed his thumb to my bottom lip, the flare of something hot and possessive in his gaze shocking me into silence. 'Renzo does not own you,' he said. 'And he's not the boy's father, I am.'

It was a low blow, one that he had used ruthlessly to dig into the knot of guilt cutting off my air supply. Suddenly he seemed more like a jealous lover staking a claim than an employer trying to lure talent away from a rival but, before I could voice my concern, he continued.

'I will buy out your contract with Camaro—and if he is truly a friend he will know this is a great opportunity he should not deny you.'

'I still can't accept. It seems like too much because it is. Be honest with me, Alexi, why are you really offering me this job—because you want me on your R&D team or because I refused the financial settlement your legal team offered me yesterday? And this is just a means to get me to take the money another way?'

I thought I had won the argument when his gaze dropped away, his stance wary and tense instead of possessive and domineering.

But, when he finally turned back to me, what I saw stunned me—not demand, or guilt, or even anger but brutal honesty.

'Can it not be for both those reasons?' he asked.

He walked back to me and touched my cheek. Even though I knew I shouldn't, I couldn't resist the urge to lean into the light caress. The wry smile that twisted his lips was both poignant and painful.

'I wish to get to know my son, and I can't do that if he lives miles away. The Galanti R&D department is based in Nice. I can buy you a villa there, pay for any staff you need and arrange to visit more frequently than I would be able to if you continued to live in London.'

I shifted my head back. Immediately the pang of

regret echoed in my abdomen as his callused palm slipped away.

'I can't accept your charity,' I said. 'And I'm not sure upending Cai's life and mine is the right way to prepare him for this relationship. It's already going to be such a big change for him and…'

His finger touched my lips again, silencing my string of objections, some of which were genuine but some of which were borne of the same cowardice that had made me keep Cai's birth a secret for so long. Alexi had always overwhelmed me, and moving back into his orbit scared me on a visceral level I did not want to admit. What if I couldn't keep at bay the feelings I was scared I still had for him? Or the desire?

'Shh…' he murmured gently. His fingertip sent inappropriate shivers down my spine as he slid it across my mouth. 'This is not charity, Belle. You have earned this opportunity. I want to develop the Galanti X to be the best car in Super League history and the key to that is fuel efficiency. To make those innovations, I need you. But this is not just about what is good for Galanti. It is also about what is good for you and your career development. You know as well as I do the Destiny team cannot offer you the resources of Galanti, or the infrastructure. If you want to be the best, you need to be employed by the best. And that's me.'

The arrogance with which he made the comment was all Alexi, but I couldn't deny that he was right. Galanti's development centre in Nice was the best in the sport, by a long margin. Probably because the company had been at the top of motor racing ever since Alexi had taken over the reins of the operation from his father seven years ago.

I'd never considered working at Galanti because of my personal attachment to Alexi, but having that golden ring dangled in front of my nose made me realise that, while protecting myself and Cai from discovery, I had been hampering my own professional development.

Strike two to my cowardice!

I'd already gone as far as I could at Camaro—if Alexi was prepared to fund additional research....

'But I also wish to support my son in any way I can,' Alexi added.

My excitement at the new job opportunity hit a brick wall as Alexi mentioned Cai.

Yes, I wanted my son to have a chance to get to know his father, especially if Alexi was willing. But Cai's whole life was based in London. That was where his friends were, his school, the teacher he adored whose class he was due to move into full time at the end of the summer. But, even as the excuses ran through my head, I knew they were just that... Excuses.

'So, are we agreed?' he asked, tilting my chin up. 'You will take the job, and relocate to Nice, so I can get to know my son?'

My skin heated. Perhaps I was making a huge mistake, agreeing to take this job, this opportunity, agreeing to relocate—because it wasn't just Alexi's relationship with Cai that was super-complicated. But

I knew I couldn't object any longer. I owed this to my son, the chance to get to know his father properly. I also owed it to Alexi after robbing him of the first four years of his son's life. And maybe I owed it to myself too. I'd worked so hard to have an opportunity like the one Alexi was offering me…

This didn't have to be about me or him. I needed to be pragmatic now. As pragmatic as Alexi had always been.

Yes, we'd kissed, and it had been phenomenal, but I was an adult with adult responsibilities—and Alexi had not suggested that he wished to take our kiss any further. Thank goodness.

Controlling my heart, as well as my hormones, where he was concerned would not be easy, but then who said life had to be easy? The important thing was I knew the risks this time. I was going into this with my eyes open.

So I nodded. 'Okay,' I said. 'I'll take the job. And bring Cai to Nice. Thank you.'

'Excellente…' he whispered.

But then he hooked a lock of hair behind my ear— and I wondered if I had just bitten off a great deal more than I would ever be able to chew.

CHAPTER SEVEN

Belle

'Wow, WOULD YOU look at this view? It's breathtaking!'
Jessie swung open the doors leading onto an elegant
balcony that wrapped around the front of our new
home. Nice stretched out below us: the wide arc of the
beach, the promenade and the warren of streets behind, like a series of treasures waiting to be explored.

'Mummy, I can see boats and a pool!' Cai shouted
gleefully, putting his small hands on the marble bal-
ustrade and lurching up onto his tiptoes to get a better view. With the city several miles away, the villa
was part of the built-up area between Nice and Ville-
franche-sur-Mer. Perched on the cliffs, it had an envi-
able parcel of private land split into terraced gardens
that included an outdoor patio area, a small, shallow
fenced-off pool complete with a water slide and a
series of steps leading down from the pool to a nar-
row inlet below us.

'And look, Mummy, a *beach*. Is that ours too?'
Probably.

'I don't know—we'll have to ask Pierre,' I said as I laid a hand on Cai's shoulder. 'Why don't you find him and invite him to lunch?'

Alexi's assistant had arranged everything over the past weeks and had been in constant contact. I'd tried to veto the more extravagant places he'd suggested, but when he'd driven us here from the airport he had explained to me that Alexi had insisted on purchasing this villa for us.

I'd been prepared to refuse Alexi's extravagance— I wanted Cai to feel at home here. He wasn't used to the kind of luxury Alexi took for granted. But as soon as Cai had seen this place—and his new bedroom, which came complete with racing-car wallpaper and a bed shaped like Galanti's latest Super League prototype—I'd realised Alexi had completely outmanoeuvred me.

I wouldn't be able to tear Cai away from here with dynamite.

But as Cai ran off through the house, shouting for Pierre like a wild thing, his excitement clear, I couldn't resent his happiness. Especially as I knew my objections to living in this palace were not really to do with Cai's reaction. Cai had always been adaptable and he loved to meet new people and see new places. He would thrive in this environment.

No, my objections were all my own, because this place felt as overwhelming as all the other sudden changes in my life.

I'd been introduced to Alexi's R&D team a week before on a brief trip to France and was enthusiastic about starting my new job. I'd taken a month off after resigning my position at Camaro to settle myself and my son into our new home, but I'd already gone over the designs for the new prototype and had attended some runs at the test track. The work would be exciting, challenging and everything Alexi had said it would be in terms of my career development.

Jessie was a personal events chef, so she had arranged to take a break between contracts to join us in Nice for the summer and help ease Cai into his new childcare situation when I started my job. I couldn't have been more grateful for her presence now as she walked towards me and gave me a brief hug.

'Is it just me, or are you totally blown away by the grandeur of this place?' she said, grinning.

'It's not just you,' I said, but I couldn't muster an answering grin.

'What's wrong?'

'It's too much,' I replied.

'I know what you mean.' Jessie scanned the palatial front parlour, taking in the ornate plasterwork on the ceilings and the luxury furniture—that I wasn't sure was going to survive Cai. I had to ensure he didn't bring his felt tip pens in here, ever.

'I've never lived somewhere like this,' she said.

'Neither have I, which is why I suspect Alexi insisted on buying it,' I said.

He hadn't listened to me. In fact, he hadn't even contacted me since the afternoon I'd agreed to relocate. 'It feels like a show of strength.'

And the irony was, he didn't need to do that. I already knew how rich and powerful he was, but until this moment I had not considered how much I had put myself at his mercy by not just agreeing to this move, but also taking the job. It was a real job, with real prospects, and Alexi and I would not be working too closely together from what I could gather. But why hadn't I even considered the implications of becoming his employee—of making him my boss?

'Perhaps,' Jessie said. But her smile didn't die, it simply became thoughtful. 'Or perhaps he's trying to impress you and Cai.'

'I don't think so,' I said. 'He hasn't even been in touch about meeting Cai since we agreed to come here.' Which I could admit now was what scared me the most. Had this ever been about establishing a relationship with his son? Or was it all some kind of power play, to let me know who was in charge? Because I felt as powerless now as I had five years ago. And I didn't like it.

Jessie grasped my hands and stroked her thumbs over my knuckles. 'Is there any reason why you can't contact him?'

The quiet question startled me with its simplicity.

Jessie was right. Why was I letting Alexi call all the shots? I'd spoken to Cai in the vaguest of terms about his father, and then waited for his father to get in touch so we could arrange some kind of plan for Cai and him to get to know each other. But no contact had been forthcoming, so I'd buried myself in finishing up my work at Camaro, organising our move, preparing Cai for his new home and new nursery school, establishing myself in the new job and waited. And waited.

No wonder I was so on edge. I still had no idea how Cai and I figured in Alexi's life, and that was my fault as much as Alexi's, because I hadn't pushed. I hadn't even asked. I'd allowed this whole thing to be managed on Alexi's timetable.

'No, there isn't,' I replied. 'Perhaps it's time I took control instead of leaving things to Alexi.'

Especially as he seemed unwilling or unable to take the initiative.

Pierre walked into the room with Cai in his arms. 'I'd love to stay for lunch, Mademoiselle Simpson. Thank you for the invitation.'

Cai giggled—he adored Pierre and the young man adored him. But it wasn't Alexi's assistant Cai had come to Nice to bond with.

As Cai and Jessie left the room to help Camille, the new housekeeper Alexi had hired for us, with the lunch preparations, I spoke to Alexi's assistant.

'Pierre, do you know where Alexi is at the moment? And how I can contact him?' As soon as I made the request, I realised exactly how much of a doormat I'd been. I didn't even have a mobile number for Alexi.

The young man's dark skin flushed even darker. 'Monsieur Galanti is coming back from Rome today. He will be at Villa Galanti tonight before he heads to London tomorrow to start preparations for the British Primo Grande Race.'

How fortunate, I thought. Just as Cai and I arrived

in France, Alexi was heading to London. It was almost as if he'd planned to make it impossible to meet his son.

He wanted me here at his beck and call, but I was increasingly becoming less convinced he even wanted to meet his son.

'Do you know where I could hire a car for Cai and I to use while we're here?' I asked.

Pierre brightened. 'There is no need to hire transportation. There are three new Galanti models in the garage at the back of the house for your use, *mademoiselle*.'

'Three!' I almost choked, yet more evidence of Alexi's skill at making me feel overwhelmed. 'Why would we need three cars?'

Pierre barely blinked. 'Monsieur Galanti thought you would need a range of cars depending on your activities. He asked me to supply you with a Galanti GLQ SUV for family excursions, a new GL8 convertible for leisure driving and a hatchback from Galanti's GLTi range of city cars in case you wish to drive into Nice or Cannes.'

I nodded. 'Right.' Apparently Alexi had thought of everything—except the most important thing, how to begin forming a relationship with his son.

Once Cai was in bed, I could leave Jessie here to babysit and drive along the coast road towards Monaco and Villa Galanti. It was less than a half-hour drive.

Surprising Alexi in person made more sense than trying to contact him.

I had uprooted my son. I wanted him finally to

meet his father—and for his father to meet him. That was why we were here. And I wanted to make the arrangements with Alexi before I began work properly at Galanti's R&D centre when the ties between our professional and personal relationship would only complicate things more.

If the mountain wasn't prepared to come to Muhammad, Muhammad was going to have to be brave enough to go to the mountain—with a little help from a brand new top-of-the-range GL8 convertible.

Night had fallen by the time I drove the new convertible—which had handled beautifully—through the gates at Villa Galanti.

Would Alexi know I was here by now? Pierre had buzzed me in and would probably be informing our boss of my visit. My nerves jumped and jiggled in my belly as I braked in front of the mansion's Belle Époque façade. I ran through the speech I'd been rehearsing during the scenic drive along the Grande Corniche and tried not to recall another summer night. If the memories had been difficult to suppress the last time I'd been here, they were impossible to suppress now.

Pierre appeared to greet me. 'Mademoiselle Simpson, we did not expect you,' he said, but he looked pleased to see me. I doubted Alexi would feel the same way.

'Is Alexi here?' I asked.

'Yes, Monsieur Galanti arrived an hour ago. He

has gone for a walk in the grounds. Would you like to wait while I inform him of your arrival?'

So Pierre hadn't told him yet. I could still surprise him. I wanted to surprise him. Alexi had always had the upper hand between us, just this once I wanted to be the one in charge... Or at least the one better prepared.

'Would it be okay if I went to find him? It's important I speak to him straight away.'

Pierre's expression became concerned and I knew he was assuming there was a problem with Cai. I didn't correct him.

'Yes, of course,' he said, whipping out his smart phone. 'Would you like me to text him and ask him to come to the house?'

'No, that's fine,' I said, my nerves twisting into a knot in my belly—I'd never been good at subterfuge. 'I can find him. I know the grounds well.'

Pierre nodded and stowed his phone as I hurried off.

I made my way through the dark gardens. The old paths and structures held so many more memories in the moonlight. I prayed that Alexi hadn't gone for an evening swim, the way I knew he had done once to de-stress. The last thing I needed was to find him semi-naked in the pool, but as I moved through the silent flowerbeds, the scent of jasmine and bougain-villea filling my senses, I heard the muffled splash-ing coming from the terrace below.

I halted, my breath catching in my lungs. I should return to the villa, confront him later, but something propelled me onwards—perhaps it was my anger with him and his avoidance of Cai and me ever since I had agreed to come to Nice. But the hum low in my abdomen which became louder and more insistent as I took the steps down to the pool terrace told a different story.

I spotted him getting out of the pool. The moonlight gilded his body, the heavy muscles and the lean sinews flexing and bunching as he grabbed a towel from a lounger. This time, I didn't wait for him to strip down further.

I was here to speak for my son, I told myself, not to satisfy the hunger that buzzed and throbbed low in my belly.

'Alexi?' My voice sounded rough as I alerted him to my presence.

His head lifted, and his gaze met mine.

If I had hoped to catch him off-guard I was sadly disappointed. He seemed as indomitable as ever and as self-assured. His gaze roamed over me—burning every inch of exposed skin it touched.

'Bella notte,' he said. 'Spying on me again?'

He threw the towel around his shoulders, giving me an unencumbered view. At thirty there was no longer even the pretence of youth or softness about him. The swimming trunks that clung to his wet thighs did nothing to disguise the hard lines and unyielding strength of his body.

'We need to talk,' I said, struggling to swallow the knot of need making my throat ache and my sex pound. 'About Cai,' I added, but the words came out on a croak.

Why did he have to be so mouth-watering?

He walked towards me, slicking his wet hair back from his forehead. The moonlight made the damp waves look so dark they were almost black. Memory stirred but the surge of heat was too real, too vivid to be merely an echo of an old desire.

Who had I been kidding? Was I really here for my son or was I here for myself? Was that the real reason I had accepted his job, his largesse, why I had uprooted my child?

'Pierre tells me the boy likes the house and his new bedroom,' he said as he approached. I was surprised by the comment. So he *had* spoken to Pierre—had he even had a hand in choosing the decor for Cai's bedroom which my son adored so much? Why had I never even considered he might have?

I caught the scent of chlorine on his wet skin. The giddy heat spiralled down to my core.

'Yes, yes he does,' I said, stumbling over the words, my gaze devouring him. 'Who chose the bed? He loves it.'

I saw the slash of colour hit his tanned cheeks and emotion swelled in my throat to go with the giddy heat.

'The designer suggested something similar,' he said. 'But I commissioned one to look like our latest prototype. I would have enjoyed such a bed as a boy. And it seemed to make sense as his mother will be working on the design.'

The thoughtfulness of the gesture made my heart thunder painfully against my ribs.

'What is the problem we need to discuss?' he said, standing so close, too close.

I knew I should step back, but the urge to feel those firm lips on mine once more was so overwhelming I felt weak with desperation. I struggled to get a grip on the conversation. To discuss his responsibilities to our son. But my reasons for being here suddenly seemed hopelessly confused. And premature. Why was I trying to force this relationship? The bed proved Alexi was thinking about his son—he wasn't ignoring him. Or avoiding him. This was as big an adjustment for him as it was for Cai. I shouldn't be here. Not when I'd clearly failed to get my hunger for him under any semblance of control.

'It doesn't matter. I should leave,' I blurted out, the flight instinct finally taking root.

But as I turned to flee he snagged my upper arm in a firm, unyielding grip.

'Don't…' The raw plea rasped across my senses, halting me in my tracks.

He tugged me round, his gaze dark with arousal as it met mine, and the hunger surged through me like a forest fire licking across my skin, and flaring deep in my sex.

'Don't go,' he said, then lifted a hand and trailed a thumb down my cheek.

I shuddered, and his pupils dilated to black.

'Tell me why you are *really* here, *bella notte*,' he said.

I was left with no choice but to tell him the truth.

Or rather, the truth I had believed until I had seen him in the moonlight.

'I wanted to find out why you haven't contacted me...' I coughed, trying to release the tightness in my throat. 'Why you haven't contacted *us*,' I corrected.

His touch trailed down to my collarbone, sending the sensations surging between my thighs. He brushed his thumb across the sensitive hollow where my pulse was hammering the skin. Could he feel it too?

I knew he could when his gaze focused on mine, so hot and devastating, seeing me and only me.

'I haven't contacted you because I knew if I saw you again too soon I would not be able to keep my hands off you,' he said, his voice as hoarse and feral as mine. And I knew, with devastating clarity, that there would be no escaping this incendiary heat a second time.

There was and always had been unfinished business between us. Business I had tried not to acknowledge for five years. But I was forced to acknowledge it now as my sex swelled, the damp heat flooding into my panties.

I wore a silk summer dress, not unlike the cocktail dress I'd worn that night. Why had I changed into it from the jeans and T-shirt I'd worn on the plane? Why had I showered and put on make-up before climbing into the car tonight?

To feel strong, to feel in control, to feel as if I were a million miles away from that unsophisticated girl. That was what I'd told myself an hour ago. But I knew that for the lie it was when his fingers curled around my neck and he tugged me closer, his breath inhaling the perfume I'd dabbed at my pulse points.

'You should not have come, *bella*,' he murmured against my neck.

I know.

The thought reverberated in my head, but I couldn't seem to regret the impulses that had driven me here any more, the lies I'd told myself.

I pressed my palms to his abdominal muscles, knowing I should push him back and step away from the fire.

He didn't try to resist my touch, simply shuddered, as if waiting for me to make the choice for both of us.

But, instead of pushing him away, my head dropped back, giving him access to my pummelling pulse.

I could barely hear the harsh Italian curse because of the pulse thundering in my ears before his lips found the sensitive spot. He kissed me, sucking, nipping, devouring the sensitive flesh between my neck and my collarbone before his mouth captured mine— swallowing my sob of surrender.

The heat rioted over my body as I caressed the contours of his naked chest. Encouraging, enticing.

It was madness, but it was a madness I could no longer control.

Why couldn't I have this just once more? I'd made a child with this man, I'd loved him once, but this was just hunger, desire. Perhaps I needed to give into it one last time to escape it for good?

If this was really why I had come to Nice, why I had driven along the coast road this evening, then maybe I owed it to myself—and my son—to get it out of my system. So we could both start concentrating on the only thing that really mattered: Cai.

Alexi's tongue delved, devouring, possessing, even more demanding than it had been the last time we'd given in to the desire. But this time I knew instinctively there would be no going back until the hunger had been sated.

He tore his mouth away, gripped my cheeks. 'Tell me you want this as much as I do.'

'Yes... I do,' I stuttered, the desire far too strong to deny.

'Bene,' he murmured, then scooped me into his arms and strode across the pool terrace.

It took me several seconds to realise what was happening, the thundering beat of my heart and the relentless heat making it hard to breathe, let alone think.

'Where are we going?' I asked.

'To my bed. I'll be damned if I take you on a lounger again,' he said, his voice harsh with frustration.

'I can walk,' I said, dazed and disorientated as he strode to the end of the terrace and up the stairs to the mansion.

'Sta'zitto.'

Shut up. *Nice,* I thought, but couldn't find the breath to say it.

All I could do was cling to him as he tightened his grip and took the steps two at a time. He carried me into the house where I had once wanted so badly to belong, and held me close as he climbed the stairs to his bedroom.

The possessiveness of his hold on me did nothing to make the riot of emotions and sensations subside.

Finally he put me down in front of the huge king-sized bed. The large room's dark upholstery and heavy furniture was intimidatingly masculine. It suited him perfectly.

'Take off the dress,' he demanded.

I obeyed, caught in the maelstrom of passion, of desire. I fumbled with the zip, let the thin silk shimmer over sensitised skin, and watched intently as he kicked off his wet swimming trunks.

His erection sprang up, hard, thick and long with a yearning he could not disguise.

'And the rest,' he murmured, nodding at my bra and panties, before grabbing a box of condoms from the bedside table.

I took off my underwear with trembling fingers, caught in the tractor beam of his gaze as he sheathed the massive erection.

The lights from Nice twinkled in the distance as I climbed onto the bed, silhouetting him through the French windows. But Nice felt like a million miles away as he joined me, cocooning us both in the unstoppable passion, the relentless desire, our ragged breathing harsh in the still night.

He pushed me back on the bed, opened my thighs and then, to my shock, moved lower to press his face between my legs.

That first slow lick as he found my clitoris with his tongue made the already out-of-control sensations sparkle and soar.

I launched off the bed, already shattering, but he held me down, drawing forth the devastating orgasm.

As my senses swelled and shattered, then rose to shatter again, the emotion I'd been trying to control gripped my chest.

'Please... I need you inside me,' I begged, shocked by my own desperation.

He rose over me, blocking out the lights, clasped my hips, notched his penis at my entrance and thrust heavily inside me.

I sobbed, the sound raw, my slick sex struggling to adjust to the all-consuming fullness, and as I gripped his thick length and clung to his wide shoulders, the pleasure swelling as he moved, I felt the emotion in my throat swell and shatter too.

CHAPTER EIGHT

Alexi

MY HEART EXPANDED in my chest as I moved inside the tight clasp of Belle's body. I still had the taste of her on my lips as I established a rhythm, digging deeper, taking more. The urgency, the drive to possess her, was so strong it controlled me instead of me controlling it.

I didn't care. In that moment, all I cared about was seeing her break again for me. Her sobs echoed in my ear, her frantic breathing spurring me on. I gritted my teeth and pumped harder, faster, felt the pleasure surge, tightening around the base of my spine like a vice.

'Come for me, again, *bella*,' I commanded, desperate to have her break once more, needing her to break first.

I was the one in control this time. I had to be.

She cried out against my ear, massaging my length, and I let go at last, the climax firing through me so raw and real it seemed to surge from my very soul.

I locked my elbows to stop myself from collapsing on top of her and letting her know how completely she'd destroyed me.

It was sex—only sex.

The chemistry had always been phenomenal between us and it seemed that had not changed.

It was five years, though, since I'd felt this exhausted, this limp from a simple orgasm. And I knew it was pointless trying to deny it any longer.

Where Belle was concerned there had always been more between us than just chemistry.

It would be good if this time we could feed the desire without guilt, but as I rolled off her, covering my face with my forearm, struggling to catch my breath before I spoke, I felt her stiffen beside me and knew we could not.

Because now, instead of Remy between us, there was the boy.

She'd come here to find out what my intentions were towards the child and perhaps it was time I admitted my misgivings about fatherhood.

She shifted, ready to run again, and I gathered enough of my energy to grasp her wrist before she could escape.

'I should leave,' she whispered, her naked body shivering. 'I need to get back to Cai.'

The room was warm, the night air sultry as it flowed in through the open doors of the terrace, the terrace on which I'd stood, thinking of her every night I'd been back to the villa since seeing her again, since that damn kiss.

'Not yet. We need to talk about the boy,' I managed to say around the sickening regret in my throat.

'I can't…' Her voice broke as she twisted her wrist free of my grasp. 'I can't talk about him now, let's talk about it tomorrow.'

She scrambled off the bed, her fear almost palpable as she gathered the clothes she had taken off with such artless seduction moments before. The moon glowed on her pale skin and I became momentarily mesmerised again. As I watched her slip on her panties, hook her bra with shaking fingers, the heat swelled my shaft again.

I forced myself to climb off the bed, walk to the chest of drawers and pull out a pair of sweat pants.

The chemistry was still there, and more volatile than ever, but I was through trying to avoid it. Trying to avoid her.

Once she had shimmied back into the simple summer dress that looked more sophisticated to me than a courtesan's ball gown, she hunted around for her sandals.

I scooped them off the floor, but as she reached for them I whisked them out of her grasp.

The moonlight shone on her face as she stared at me. I could see the beginnings of beard burn on her cheeks where I had devoured her mouth before devouring so much else. The taste of her—sweet and musky, wet with need—taunted me still.

'Please, Alexi, I have to go,' she said desperately, but I could hear her struggle to keep the fear out of her voice. 'I can't...' A guilty flush burned her neck. 'This shouldn't have happened—it's not why I came here.'

We both knew on some level that was a lie. Maybe her decision hadn't been conscious, any more than mine had been to avoid the boy simply so I could avoid her too, but that cat was out of the bag now, and there would be no shoving it back in again. Even so, I needed to be careful with her.

She looked freaked out. I wondered again at her experience. How could she still seem like that young, artless girl when she was the mother of a child, *my* child?

'Maybe, but you did come here, so perhaps it is best we discuss the reason why. Do you want me to have more contact with the boy?' I asked.

'It's okay,' she said. 'I understand now why you've been avoiding us. I should have—'

'No, you don't,' I interrupted.

She'd apologised before, but she hadn't been wrong about my reasons for avoiding contact, not entirely. Perhaps it was time I took some share of the blame for my son's fatherless existence.

'Yes, I do,' she said. 'You wanted to avoid...' She gesticulated with her hands between us, in an entirely inadequate expression of the explosion of hormones and pheromones, wants and needs held in a pressure cooker for five years, that had just occurred. 'You wanted to avoid this happening again. After that kiss, I should have realised we couldn't be in the same space again without a chaperone, and yet I came up here anyway to...'

'Shh, Belle.' I pressed a thumb to her lips to silence the words and the anguish and guilt behind them. 'What happened was inevitable,' I said. 'Avoiding you and my responsibilities to the boy was never going to stop that.'

'Of course it wasn't inevitable,' she said, her face alight with panic and indignation. 'We had a choice and we took the wrong one. Again.'

I had to stifle a harsh laugh at her naivety, even though I found it strangely endearing. Surely she could not have slept with many men since me, if she didn't know how rare was the chemistry we shared?

'It wasn't the wrong choice then,' I said. 'Because it gave us our son.'

And as far as I was concerned it wasn't the wrong choice now either. I wanted her, I had wanted her for five years, and I was through trying to avoid it. Especially as I could suddenly see my avoidance had as much to do with my fear of fatherhood as it did with my fear of losing control with her.

I could see I had struck her dumb, so I continued.

'I *was* scared,' I said, forcing the words out past the lump of denial in my throat. I hated to admit a weakness, hated to admit I'd ever been afraid, but for once it made sense to let her see this was much more of a struggle than I had let on. 'Scared of being a father. That's the other reason I avoided contacting you.'

She didn't say anything, her eyes going wide and making her look even more delicious.

My erection throbbed under the loose sweats but I

ignored it. We would not have a repeat performance tonight, not until she had come to terms with the idea.

If I wanted to have Belle again—and I now knew I did—I needed to get past my fear of fatherhood.

'I never intended to have a child and I'm fairly sure, given my past record, I will be incredibly bad at it.'

'Your...' She swallowed, her eyes shadowed with a grief I didn't understand. 'Your past record? You mean you have other children?'

'*Dio*, no!' I barked out a strained laugh. 'You are the only woman I have failed to protect so spectacularly,' I murmured.

You are also the only woman who has made me forget everything but the driving need to be inside you.

I bit off the admission. That would not continue to be the case once we had fed this hunger. Nothing ever lasted, especially not physical desire—it was transient, fleeting—but for us, I suspected, the intensity was increased by all the other commitments we shared, to the dead and to the living, to the past and the future.

There was no way to disentangle ourselves unless we faced the truth instead of running from it. We'd both done our fair share of that—she'd had a child and refused to tell me of his existence for five years, but I had also refused to see the truth about my own brother and refused to meet my son.

We had both been cowards about so much. The only way forward now was to be brave. And, if that meant admitting weaknesses I did not wish to admit so I could work past them, so be it.

Facing those realities meant I would be able to feed this hunger instead of trying to deny it, which was one hell of an incentive to stop running.

'Then what past record are you talking about?' she asked.

'I failed my brother. I failed you,' I said, forcing the words past the guilt which I had deflected and denied for so long. 'I do not wish to fail the boy too…'

CHAPTER NINE

Belle

I STARED AT Alexi and blinked furiously to hold back the sting of tears at his honesty—and the hopelessness I suspected lay behind it.

Did he really believe he would be a bad father? He hadn't failed Remy, and he hadn't really failed me. He'd been cruel to me that day, but he'd been grief-stricken at the time—we both had.

But, as the emotion closed my throat, I knew I couldn't have this discussion now. My sex was still tender, my face alight with shame and shock and my pulse had accelerated to a mile a minute.

I needed to get away from him, from here, to take stock, to make sure I didn't fall into his arms again—and unleash all those destructive emotions that had tripped me up before.

I was terrified of my feelings for him—confused as they were. They felt too strong to be merely echoes of my former childish adoration.

I couldn't afford to fall in love with him again.

Alexi had always been a hard man to love. I hadn't realised it as a girl, blinded by all the qualities I adored—his protectiveness, his dominance, his determination. But I could see now how destructive those qualities could be for me, as well as how attractive.

I'd never known my own father, who had died soon after I was born, and as a result I'd spent my childhood looking for male approval. The more unattainable Alexi had become, the more I'd wanted him. He was just as unattainable now. I needed to figure out how to handle discovering my body was still enthralled by him, and only him.

And I needed to figure it out quickly, before I told Cai who Alexi was.

And before I started my new job in his organisation.

We would always have a connection now, but I couldn't let it become a sexual one. I had thought I was invulnerable to his charms. I had just discovered that I was not. Managing our emotional commitments was going to be hard enough already, but adding this explosive sexual connection would turn them into a minefield.

'Being a parent isn't something you're instinctively good or bad at,' I managed at last. 'It's something you have to learn. I was terrified I'd fail Cai as soon as he was born. Even before he was born,' I admitted. 'And I still make mistakes now. In fact, I've made some humdingers. Not telling his father he existed being the most obvious one.'

'Perhaps it is time you stopped beating yourself up about that.' He shoved his fists into the pockets of his sweat pants. They hung low on his hips, only making me more aware of the muscular expanse of his bare chest.

I looked away, something releasing inside me at the offhand demand.

'Thank you for not hating me,' I said.

'You were very young,' he murmured. 'And I behaved badly towards you.'

His knuckle touched my chin, forcing my gaze to meet his.

'If you were so terrified of becoming a mother, why did you decide to keep the child?' he asked.

Because I loved you so much, too much.

The words echoed in my head. But I couldn't say them because they would make me even more vulnerable than I was already. That he would never have suspected the truth seemed to damn those feelings even more. And made me realise how futile they had always been.

'I guess I wasn't thinking much. I'm not even sure I made a conscious decision. I was too confused. Too heartsick after Remy's death and…' *And being banished by you*, I thought but didn't add. 'And having to leave Monaco and my life here. And then, once I'd seen his tiny form on the first scan, there was only one choice that felt right for me.'

It wasn't the whole truth, but it was enough of the truth to satisfy him, because he nodded and tucked his hands back into his pockets.

'But I'm sorry I took the choice away from you,' I said, even though I wasn't sorry, because I could never be sorry for having Cai. 'Of whether or not to become a father.' I sucked in a lungful of air. I really needed to go now—this was getting awkward and too much. 'I think we should take time out. There's no pressure for you to meet Cai. It's a big adjustment for him coming to Nice and it'll take a while for him to settle. And it's obviously a big adjustment for you too. I want you both to be ready.'

It was a lie. Cai was a remarkably adaptable child and I already knew he would make himself right at home in our new palace. But I couldn't face Alexi again for a while. I needed time, space and distance. The hunger still hummed in my sex, and I couldn't seem to get any of this into perspective.

I picked my sandals off the top of the dresser where he'd placed them and slipped them on. He was still staring at me, and I had the weirdest sensation he could see right through my show of maturity to the panicked girl beneath.

'Why don't I give you a call once Cai's properly settled, in a couple of weeks, and we can arrange some visitation—if that works for you?'

He frowned. 'A couple of weeks?'

'Well, yes,' I mumbled. 'Pierre said you're headed to the UK tomorrow to prep for the Primo Grande,' I said, suddenly desperately thankful for that piece of fortuitous timing. The British super race was several weeks away. It would give me time to get over this insistent, dangerous hunger. 'It would be much better if, when you meet him for the first time, you don't then have to then disappear for weeks.' I carried on talking as I walked backwards towards the door, scared he would try to stop me again. And even more scared that I wanted him to. 'A week to a four-year-old is an eternity. So why don't we leave it until you get back?'

He didn't answer, but I took his silence as his consent.

'Great,' I said and left.

I ran down the stairs, out the back door and climbed into the convertible. But, as the powerful car purred to life, I couldn't resist glancing over my shoulder.

My breath caught as I spotted him, standing on the veranda of his bedroom, watching me.

I accelerated into the night, swallowing down the burst of heat—and fear.

CHAPTER TEN

Alexi

AFTER RINGING THE bell the following morning at the door of the villa I had purchased for Belle and my son, I pushed my hands into my pockets and waited for her to answer.

My heart galloped into my throat and heat settled at the base of my spine as I heard footsteps inside the house and a female voice.

'Just a minute.'

The door swung open, but the tension in my gut relaxed. The woman in front of me wasn't Belle. She looked vaguely familiar, though. She had the same heart-shaped face as Belle, her hair a deep chestnut instead of the rich vibrant red of Belle's. Pretty, but not stunning. I decided the woman must be the second cousin I had met briefly in Barcelona when my life had changed for ever.

'Hi,' she said, looking surprised and then gifting me with a brilliant smile that made her look surprisingly pleased to see me and turned her pretty features into something more.

I tensed, instantly suspicious.

I had been prepared for a frosty reception from Belle and her cousin this morning, and possibly my son too. They were not expecting me, but as I'd watched the lights on Belle's car disappearing into the darkness yesterday I'd made a few important decisions. As a result, I'd spent two hours this morning rearranging my schedule for the next three weeks so I could remain most of the time in Monaco.

I was here not just to face up to my responsibilities concerning the boy but also to apprise Belle of one important fact. She could no longer keep me out of his life, or hers. I'd seen the panic in her expressive eyes the night before, and had realised her suggestion that I wait weeks more to introduce myself to my son had nothing to do with the child's welfare and everything to do with the events in my bedroom.

'It's Mr Galanti, isn't it?' the woman said, offering her hand as I stepped inside. 'My name's Jessie Burton. I'm Belle's cousin—we met in Barcelona but I doubt you'll remember me,' she added as she shook my hand in a firm grip. 'You had eyes only for Belle that day, and Cai.' She continued to beam, apparently not upset I had ignored her. 'Come through to the terrace,' she said, as she let go of my hand and led me into the house. 'Belle and Cai are having breakfast.'

As I stepped into the main living area, I spotted Belle and my son seated at the table on the *terrazza*. The panoramic view of Nice behind them was quite spectacular, and one of the reasons I had insisted on this house for them, but it wasn't the view that had the air clogging my lungs. The cousin, whose name I'd already forgotten, was still chatting about something but her words faded, my heartbeat pounding in my eardrums. I hesitated as the blast of longing blindsided me the way it had the night before....and so many other nights before that.

Spotlighted in the morning sun, Belle wore a simple pair of summer shorts and a T-shirt, her wild hair tied back in a tidy ponytail. But even in the simple, tomboyish attire she looked exquisite as she chuckled at something the boy had said.

And so young—not old enough to have a child. Not old enough to have made love to me with such unbridled passion last night.

'Belle, we have a surprise guest for breakfast,' the cousin called out as she approached the table.

The little boy's dark head whipped round and his eyes, so like Remy's, locked on mine. 'Who is he?' he said bluntly.

But it was his mother's reaction which made the heat pulse low in my abdomen.

She stiffened, clearly shocked by my appearance, and then the colour on her cheeks—devoid of make up this morning which made the sprinkle of freckles look all the more delicious—flared.

'Alexi?' she murmured, clearly not as pleased to see me as her cousin.

The boy, who had scrambled down from his chair, ran towards me.

'Who are you?' he asked as he reached me.

He stood with his small fists perched on his hips and his chin thrust out.

Wearing a pair of pyjamas, decorated with a cartoon sports car with a smiling face, the child should have looked cute but instead he looked fierce, his compact body rigid with tension, his expression wary and his stance oddly confrontational. Clearly, he didn't remember meeting me all those weeks ago.

'Why are you here?' the child demanded.

A smile creased my lips despite the tension in my own belly.

The boy was defending his mother.

'Cai, you mustn't speak to Mr Galanti so rudely.' The cousin stepped in, placing her hands on the boy's shoulders.

'Mr Galanti is…' the cousin began, and then stopped and swung her head round to Belle for guidance, who sat stiffly at the table, still struck dumb by my appearance.

Realisation dawned at the cousin's hesitation. So Belle hadn't told my son of our relationship.

Irritation gripped my insides. Was she still trying to keep him from me?

It was a struggle to keep my tone even and non-confrontational as I knelt down to introduce myself to the child.

'My name is Alexi Galanti.' I lifted my gaze to Belle who had finally got over her shock and was walking towards us.

The look on her face said it all—guilt, regret and panic.

The panic could only be from one fear—that I would introduce myself to the child as his father before he was ready.

My irritation increased. But I clamped down on it.

I should have taken charge of this situation a lot sooner.

'I am a friend of your mother's,' I told the boy, repeating what we had told him all those weeks ago in Barcelona. Perhaps it was less of a lie now than it had been then.

Although, 'friend' was far too simple and straightforward a term for what Belle and I shared.

'I would like to be your friend too,' I added.

The boy's eyes widened, but instead of replying to me he glanced at his mother. 'Mummy, you said I'm not supposed to talk to strangers. Can I talk to him?'

I had to admire his bluntness and his brutal honesty, even as part of me died inside at the word 'strangers'.

The reality of the situation hit home. This boy was my son, my own flesh and blood. His Galanti heritage was evident in every part of him—not just the dark, wavy hair, the shape of his face, the pure blue eyes so like my brother's, but also in his directness, his boldness, his bravery, his determination to stand up for his mother. The way I had once tried to stand up for mine.

And because of Belle's and my mistakes, our fears,

our weaknesses, our selfishness, I could not claim him today.

Belle knelt beside the boy and banded an arm around his waist to tug him against her side. His arm wrapped around her neck, his attachment to her somehow making the regret and the longing grip my chest even harder.

In that moment, I made a promise to myself. No more running. No more hiding. For my sins, I could not claim my son today, but I would do everything in my power to make sure I could claim him soon. Very soon.

'It's okay, Cai,' Belle said softly, her voice breaking with an emotion that I could feel echoing in my own chest. 'You did the right thing to check with me first,' she said and the boy beamed, basking in his mother's praise. 'But Alexi's right, he isn't a stranger...' Her throat moved as she swallowed and I could see the sheen of moisture in her eyes. This was as hard for her as it was for me. My irritation eased a little bit. 'He *is* my friend. And I think it would be lovely if he could become your friend as well.'

The surge of possessiveness surprised me.

I wasn't the boy's friend. I was his father. And I wasn't Belle's friend either. I was her lover.

I knew I would need to hold back my fierce determination to claim the boy until I had learned a lot more about being a parent.

But I would be damned if I would pretend not to be more than a friend to Belle, especially after last night.

Our gazes met over the boy's head and the blush

on her pale cheeks flared. Awareness bristled in the air between us.

'Do you have a car, Mr Alexi?' the little boy asked, forcing my attention back to him. The smile he sent me lit his whole face—and displayed a pair of captivating dimples. 'I love cars.'

The child's serious, cautious expression had disappeared. My heartbeat slowed as memories of Remy bombarded me. My son was a complete charmer, with the same sunny disposition my brother had always possessed... Sweet and uncomplicated, more than a little cocky and unfailingly optimistic. How foolish I had been to be so scared of getting to know him, when in many ways I knew him already... And had missed him terribly.

'I own several cars,' I said, an idea occurring to me. 'Do you like racing cars?' I asked, already well aware of the answer to that question after our brief meeting in Barcelona.

The boy nodded enthusiastically, his eyes widening. 'Yes, I love racing cars the best of all.'

I decided to use his enthusiasm to my advantage. So many things about this child were familiar to me, but I was not familiar to him. I wanted that to change, and soon—so why not use every weapon in my arsenal to win the boy over?

'I own some racing cars,' I said and the little boy gasped—his excitement so innocent and unfettered it was all the more endearing.

'Really?' he said.

I nodded, his awestruck expression a sop to my battered ego.

'Perhaps you and your mother would like to come to the Galanti test track today,' I said. 'And you can sit in our latest prototype?'

The boy began to jump up and down, his excitement no longer containable. 'Can we, Mummy? Can we? *Pleeeease?*'

It was beneath me, but a part of me couldn't help being pleased that at the very least I had managed to best Camaro's offer of a month ago. I wasn't in competition with Renzo for the boy's affections, any more than I was for his mother's affections, but still I could not deny the triumphant feeling in my chest.

'Yes, of course,' Belle said. 'Jessie can go with you both. I have to stay here to…' She paused, trying to come up with a plausible excuse not to accompany us, I had no doubt.

Lifting off my knee, I stood up and held out a hand to haul her up too.

'Perhaps Jessie would like to take my…' I began, but then paused as Belle's fingers jerked in mine. I had been about to reveal my relationship to the child. 'To take Cai,' I corrected myself, 'to get dressed, and we can talk?'

'I'm not sure that's necessary…' She tugged her fingers loose, but her cousin interrupted.

'Come on, Cai,' she said, gripping the child's hand. 'Let's get you dressed so you can see the new car. And your mummy and Mr Galanti can talk,' she added pointedly.

The look that passed between the two women was not lost on me. Clearly Jessie wanted us to talk too. I decided I liked the woman a great deal.

'Can we go right now?' the child asked.

'We can go as soon as you are dressed,' I said.

'Thank you, Mr Alexi,' he said. 'I like being your friend,' he added, the innocent remark making my chest ache.

'It's just Alexi,' I called after him as he dragged Belle's cousin towards his bedroom in his rush to get changed.

As soon as Jessie and my son disappeared down the hallway, the room fell silent.

The delightful flush on Belle's cheeks had spread to engulf her collarbone. I noticed the pink rash on her neck where I'd sucked the pulse point less than ten hours ago—and driven her wild.

The heat surged back into my pants.

'I… We weren't expecting you today, but if you want to take Cai for a trip to the track I have no objections,' she said breathlessly. 'Jessie can accompany you. I've still got a ton of things to do here.'

That all sounded very reasonable, but the pulse punching her neck gave her away. She was still running, and still kidding herself we could conquer this need with denial.

I placed my hand on her neck and ignored the flash of panic. She stiffened but didn't draw away.

'Surely we discovered last night the time for cowardice is over, *bella notte*,' I said, stroking my thumb across the pulse in her collar bone, feeling it flutter uncontrollably.

'I don't know what you mean,' she said, but I could see she knew exactly what I meant. Her desire for me was the one thing she had never been able to hide.

'Then let me demonstrate,' I said as I lowered my head to hers. 'I'm not here just to claim my son,' I murmured. Her lips parted under mine with a gasp. The invitation was all the more beguiling because I was sure it was completely instinctive. 'I'm here to claim you too.'

CHAPTER ELEVEN

Belle

I'M HERE TO claim you too.

The gruff words, so sure, so dominant and so possessive, shot through me as Alexi's lips captured mine.

The dark, insistent need I had been trying to rationalise, minimise and explain all through my sleepless night leapt out of the shadows and sent glittering light cascading through my body.

My mouth opened instinctively to let him in, my fingers fisting in the soft cotton of his polo shirt as his tongue probed—demanding, relentless. He thrust deep into my mouth, exploring the recesses, tasting me again the way he had tasted me last night, but in the bright light of morning my response felt somehow more devastating, more out of control.

His hands cupped my cheeks as he angled my head for better access, his tongue delving deeper, not just claiming me but branding me.

My breathing sped up with my heart rate but my

dazed mind—which was still reeling from the shock of having Alexi in my home unannounced, and seeing him engage with our son with surprising sensitivity—managed to engage.

Why was he really here? To become a father to his son, or to reopen the Pandora's box I had tried to slam shut after last night?

I flattened my palms against his waist and managed to gather the strength to override the need and shove him back.

'Stop!' The words came out on a sob. He let me go instantly.

Perhaps he was as shocked by the incendiary nature of our physical connection as I was. But he didn't look shocked, he looked indomitable, as I stumbled back, desperate to get away from the fire still burning in my blood.

'We can't… We can't go there again.' I dragged shaking fingers through my hair, scrambling around for the right words, the right tone—calm and assured rather than weak and needy. Not easy when my heart was racing faster than the Galanti X on the final lap at the Monaco Primo Grande. I gulped down several steadying breaths.

'Why can't we, if we both want to?' he asked, his voice so assured, so reasonable, I suddenly wanted to slap him.

I shoved my fists into the pockets of my shorts to control the urge, but the switch from shock and need to anger finally helped to get my racing heartbeat past the finishing line.

'Because this…' I jerked my hand out of my pocket and flapped my palm between him and me. 'This *thing* between us isn't just about us any more.' I ground the words out, the righteous indignation for my son helping to keep the destructive desire at bay at last. 'There's a child involved. And things are confusing enough for him already. You came here this morning without consulting with me.' I'd tried to be forgiving about that, to understand. But his surprise appearance this morning was starting to look more and more like another of his power plays.

'I told you he needed more time. I haven't even had a chance to tell him who you are yet, to prepare him, and…'

'Stop it.' He grabbed my wrist and held it down, forcing my gaze to his. 'Stop pretending this is about the boy when you know it's not. You've had more than enough time to speak to him about me—four years, to be precise—but you have chosen not to. I'm not waiting any longer to get your permission to speak to my son.'

The sharp judgement in his voice, and the incontrovertible truth behind it, struck me like a blow, and the burning anger in my belly imploded, drowned by the black hole of guilt.

He let go of my wrist.

'Do you think I don't know how complicated this is?' he demanded, his voice rough now—not with judgement but with something a great deal rawer than that. 'Do you think I don't know how confusing it is—for him as well as me?'

He dragged in several breaths and I could almost feel the pain in his lungs as he did so, because mine felt the same. 'Do you think telling him I want to be his friend was easy for me, when what I want to do is tell him I'm his father?' He whispered the words, and I realised he was keeping his voice down so Cai wouldn't hear him. 'Do you think I don't know I have to earn the right to call myself that? And how hard that is going to be for me when I have no idea how to even talk to a four-year-old, let alone how to be a parent to one?'

A tear slipped over my lid—the tears I'd struggled to contain earlier when I'd watched him kneel in front of his son so he could look him in the eye, instinctively knowing how not to intimidate him. Even in that brief encounter Alexi had engaged with Cai so effortlessly—using their shared love of racing cars to start bonding with him. But I realised now, as I should have realised ten minutes ago, that none of that encounter had been effortless, at least not for Alexi.

I scrubbed the tear away, looking down at my bare feet. So ashamed.

I'd apologised to Alexi for the years of silence, for failing to tell him about his son, and I'd meant it—but how could I ever be forgiven? How could I even forgive myself until I put his needs and Cai's needs ahead of my own?

'Actually you did very well,' I said, hitching in a breath and willing myself to hold the emotion at bay. Had a part of me even been a little jealous that Alexi had bonded with Cai so easily? I had denied my son his father for so long perhaps it was time I acknowledged one of my reasons for doing so had been my own insecurities as a mother. I'd had Cai when I had been nineteen years old. I'd been a confused, terrified child myself in many ways. I'd worked long and hard to build up my confidence. I was proud of what I'd achieved, but had a part of me been scared to test that, scared to share Cai with his father, because it might illuminate my inadequacies as a mother?

This wasn't a competition, but I had made it one.

'I suspect it helps that I own a Super League team,' he said wryly, and my heart broke more—because, beneath the irony, I could hear the insecurity.

'It doesn't hurt,' I said, forcing a smile to my lips. 'But it was more than that. The way you spoke to him was very…' I gulped, trying to shrink the boulder in my throat at his inquisitive expression. 'It was really…' I wanted to say sweet, but sweet wasn't a word you could use to describe Alexi Galanti. Even as a father. It was too ordinary, too shallow, too trite. 'It was really touching,' I managed. 'It was as if you already understood him. I think you might be a natural.'

He frowned then huffed out a bitter laugh. 'I find that unlikely, given my own upbringing.'

The remark sounded flippant, but I knew it was not—he was talking about his fractured relationship with his own father. I realised what he had said to me last night, about his fear of fatherhood, wasn't just wound up in his misplaced guilt over Remy's death but also in all the cruel things his father had

said and done to him during so much of his childhood and adolescence.

All those nasty jibes, the shouted threats and criti-
cisms, the back-handed slaps and drunken punches
that Remy and I had overheard... Alexi had always
dismissed them, had always seemed immune, his confidence unbowed by his father's abuse, but that treatment had taken its toll in ways of which I had been
unaware until now.

'You were never like him, Alexi,' I said.

His frown deepened. The momentary flash of tor-
ment at the mention of his father was quickly masked
but I knew the remark had hit home. Or at least I
hoped it had, and I was glad. Because I could see
now I hadn't just robbed my son of a father over the
last four years, I had stopped this man from discovering how much better he was than his own father.

'I'm glad this first meeting went well,' he said.
'But I will need your help to ensure I don't make
mistakes.'

I nodded. 'You have it.'

He nodded back. 'I would like to be able to tell
Cai who I really am as soon as possible,' he continued. 'But I am prepared to take your lead on that, as
you know him best.'

It was a huge concession. I understood that, just
as I now understood the significance of him not announcing the truth as soon as he had arrived this
morning. He had trusted me, and now I needed to
prove to him I wasn't going to abuse that trust.

'Thank you, let's see how it goes. But Cai's actually very adaptable,' I admitted. 'He's already loving it here. And he…he's always craved male attention,' I added, thinking of how quickly he'd attached himself to Renzo and Pierre.

Why had I never noticed that before for what it was? Especially as I had yearned for a father myself through so much of my childhood.

'He's already thrilled to bits that I'm working for you…because apparently Galanti make "the bestest racing cars ever",' I added with a smile, quoting our son.

'He's a smart boy.' Alexi's eyes sparkled with amusement. 'And handsome and exceptionally self-assured. He reminds me so much of Remy at that age, it is almost uncanny.' He sobered, the frown reappearing between his brows. 'You have my word, Belle, that I will do everything in my power not to hurt him.'

My heart galloped into my throat at the sincerity in his voice.

And two things occurred to me at once: that although he was unaware of it Alexi, who guarded his heart so fiercely, had already lost it to his son and how selfish and immature I had been to believe even for a minute, let alone five years, that Alexi would not be a good father to our child when he had been such a good brother to Remy.

'I know,' I said, realising the only way I could undo the damage I had caused by keeping my secret was to support and encourage Alexi as much as I could now.

'But now we must talk of the other elephant in the room,' Alexi said.

He cupped my cheek and the buzz in my stomach ignited all over again. His thumb trailed across my lips, lips still tender from his kiss.

'What elephant?' I asked, my voice husky enough to sandpaper one of the luxury yachts anchored in the bay.

Alexi's lips quirked into a sensual smile. And I knew he could hear the husky invitation in my voice too. 'I still want you, Belle, and you want me. And I see no reason for us not to satisfy this burning hunger for each other while I learn how to be a father to our son.'

'We…we can't.' I stepped back, desperate to break the spell he could so easily weave around me. His hand dropped away but I could still feel the warmth of his palm, the roughness of the callused skin against my cheek.

'You said this before, but you didn't give me an answer. Why can't we?' he asked. There was no aggression, only mild curiosity, as if he were dealing with a skittish mare who needed to be handled gently but firmly.

'I did give you an answer. We can't, because it would be too confusing for Cai.'

'Why would it be confusing for him? We have already told him we're friends. It is not as if we would be making love in front of him,' he said.

'He's only just met you. I don't think…' I began, but he silenced me with a touch.

'You must trust me, Belle. I will not neglect him. When I am with him, my focus will be on him. My relationship with him is not dependent on my relationship with you.'

I already knew this to be true from his impassioned response a moment ago.

'Okay, but I still think it'll be too much having him know we're a couple...'

'Why will it?' he persisted. 'Surely you must have taken other men to your bed in the last four years? How did you explain them to our son?' I heard the distinct edge in his voice but ignored it. How could he possibly be jealous when he was the one who had discarded me? And, anyway, there was nothing to be jealous of. I had never taken any other men to my bed.

'I... I didn't,' I said. 'I mean, Cai never met any of them,' I added, hating the need to lie. But how could I tell Alexi he was the only man I had ever slept with when he was already behaving like a cave man? 'I always kept my sex life separate from our home life, precisely so he wouldn't get confused. I didn't want him becoming attached to someone as a father figure who would not be a permanent part of my life.'

'That does not apply here, though, does it?' he said, and I suddenly realised my lie had allowed him neatly to outmanoeuvre me. 'I am not a father *figure*—I am his father. I will always have an attachment to him, no matter whether we are sleeping together or not, so there's no reason to keep our liaison a secret from him. Or for us not to pursue this hunger in the hours we have alone together.'

'What—what hours?' I said, stammering as he pressed his palm to my cheek again. I could not hide the shudder of reaction. 'You're a busy man, and I need to be focused on getting Cai settled here before I start a demanding new job in three weeks' time…' I was babbling now, his touch making my heartbeat race and my pulse sink deep into my sex as he stroked my cheek. His hand strayed to my neck, his thumb rubbing the thundering pulse in my collar bone.

'I have cleared my schedule for the next few weeks—let's see what happens,' he murmured, before placing a possessive kiss on my lips.

My breath shuddered out, my mouth opening to accept so much more, my surrender complete. But he drew back at the sound of Cai's footsteps running back down the corridor.

'I'm ready!' Cai shouted as he appeared. But then he stopped and tilted his head to one side. 'Mummy, your face is all red,' he announced in the way children have of stating the obvious. 'Why?'

I pressed my hands to my cheeks, my face igniting even more at Alexi's smile. His large hand settled on the small of my back, making me feel owned, before he pressed a kiss to my temple.

'I just kissed your mummy,' he said. 'I hope you don't mind,' he added, asking my son's permission in a way that made my heart squeeze painfully in my chest.

'Yuck, I hate kissing,' Cai replied. 'It's so boring.'

I found myself choking out a laugh alongside Alexi's deep chuckle.

'You may change your mind about that when you're older,' Alexi announced, recovering his cool a lot quicker than I could. 'But enough talk of boring stuff,' he added, folding his son's small hand in his. 'Let's go check out the new Galanti X.'

Jessie appeared with Cai's coat and a bag full of toys just in case he got bored during the trip, something I suspected was unlikely, as he stared at his father with something akin to hero worship in his eyes.

As they made their way to the door, Jessie excused herself, neatly manoeuvring me into going with Alexi instead. A part of me still wanted to object, but Alexi sent me a look that clearly said he had no intention of letting me retreat behind my 'it's too confusing for Cai' shell again.

And I realised the only way to convince him I wasn't running any more was to go with them both today.

No man had ever staked a claim on me in front of my son.

And, even if they had, I doubt they would have been able to do it in such a way that made Cai feel more secure instead of less so.

The decision as to whether we took this 'thing' between us further was still mine. But I couldn't use Cai as a cover any more. As well as not being an answer, avoidance was no longer an option.

Alexi wouldn't allow it to be an option. So I pulled on my big girl panties and took my son's other hand as we made our way out of the house to Alexi's car.

Cai swung between us. As his sturdy little body lifted into the air, my heart swooped and swung with him, and my gaze met Alexi's.

This day would be a new experience for all three of us. We weren't a family, but we were both Cai's parents, and that was all that mattered today.

CHAPTER TWELVE

Alexi

I BRAKED THE car in front of Belle and Cai's villa as the sun dipped towards the horizon. Swinging my head round, I spotted Belle in the back seat, her head propped against the window, her eyes shut. Our son sat in the car seat beside her, his small head lolling to one side.

A smile spread up my chest to my lips at the sight of them both fast asleep. It had been an exhausting day. But I had discovered several important lessons about being a father, or even simply being a friend to a four-year-old. Their energy seemed to operate on a scale of ten or zero—full-on or fast asleep—and there was no in between. The questions never ended and could be repeated on a loop. I'd answered everything, from what was my favourite animal to why I liked racing cars, not once but approximately four hundred times.

The other thing I had discovered was that Belle was a magnificent mother. All her attention had been focused on the boy today, checking that he was okay, answering the questions I could not, directing him in everything from manners to personal safety with an ease that was always thoughtful, patient and never unkind.

The car's engine purred to a stop as I turned off the ignition.

Belle's eyelids fluttered open, the rich emerald instantly alert. 'We're here. I'm sorry. I must have drifted off,' she murmured, her voice thick with sleep. Would she sound like that when she awoke in the morning? The pheromones that were never silent buzzed back to life. I ignored them, as I had done all day.

'It's been a tiring day,' I said.

'It must have been a baptism of fire for you,' she said, sending me a rare unguarded smile. My heart skipped at the thought of how much I had missed that smile. I'd seen it several times today whenever Cai had done something funny, silly or simply enthusiastic—and every time it had had the same effect on my heart rate—but this was the first time it had been directed at me.

'Cai's pretty full-on,' she added. 'Especially when he's excited. But you were wonderful with him. I hope you know he hero worships you now?'

Her praise was as genuine and unguarded as her smile.

'I'm sure it's normal for any active four-year-old,' I murmured, at least one thing I could now say with some authority.

'Thank you,' she said, then stretched her arms up in a yawn. It made her T-shirt stretch over her full breasts. The spike of heat hit me hard. 'For making today so fun for him…' she finished.

The spike of heat was followed by a spike of irritation.

'I'm his father—why wouldn't I?' I asked.

'Of course,' she said, the guilt shadowing her eyes again.

I wanted to snatch the words back. 'Now it's my turn to be sorry,' I said.

'Why?' she asked, those mossy eyes widening. 'You have every right to be angry with me for creating this situation.'

'No, I don't,' I said firmly. 'And, anyway, that's not why I snapped at you.'

'Why did you, then?' she asked, with that artlessness which still confused me.

I let my gaze roam down to her breasts and immediately felt the sexual tension snap between us before lifting my gaze. 'Because being this close to you all day and not being able to touch you has been an exercise in frustration.'

The blush flooded her face, reddening her pale skin and illuminating her freckles in the half-light from the setting sun. She chewed her lip. 'Oh,' she said in that husky tone of voice which told me I wasn't the only one who had been frustrated.

'But that is my cross to bear,' I added, just in case she assumed I was blaming her for not being able to control my own libido. 'Not yours.'

I climbed out of the car and opened the passenger door on Cai's side. As I unhooked the harness on his child seat, she appeared beside me. She was still flushed, but when she spoke she didn't sound so wary, which I considered a good thing.

'I can carry him,' she said.

'I would like to,' I replied.

She drew back and I could see she was torn, as she had been on occasion all through the day. Giving me a piece of our son's care was hard for her, I realised. But I didn't resent her reluctance any more. He was precious cargo, and she was only protecting him, like a mother bear. The last four years or so must have been hard for her. Caring for a child was not easy.

'I swear I will not drop him,' I added, forcing a smile to my lips.

She smiled back. 'I know.'

As I lifted his slumbering body out of the car seat, a strange emotion washed over me. Protective, possessive but also filled with a strength of feeling I had never had before.

I had picked him up a few times during the day—lifting him into the Galanti X model we had come to see at the test track, later at the restaurant we had gone to for lunch and at the beach, where he had run for hours, letting me chase him as he'd shrieked. But this time was somehow different, as he lifted tired arms around my neck and snuggled into my embrace. I held him against my chest as the feeling spread and felt the sting of something in my eyes...

Could it be tears? Surely that was ludicrous? I

never cried—even as a child, when my father had taken a belt to me, when my mother had left my brother and me, or as a man when I had stood over my brother's grave...

I could feel Belle's eyes on me, so I gently shut the car door and swallowed down the rush of strange emotions. But I couldn't seem to stop myself from folding my arms securely around the boy's sturdy body and breathing in his childish scent of sweat, sea salt and the chocolate ice-cream that stained the front of his T-shirt.

As we walked together into the house, Belle rushing to open the door in front of me, the boy's head finally stirred. He lifted his eyes to mine as I stepped into their new home.

'Hello, Mr Alexi,' he said sleepily.

'Hello,' I replied, impossibly moved by the fact his arms only tightened around my neck. He wasn't scared of me. He felt safe, secure. Even after only a day in my company, he trusted me. I swore to myself never to abuse that trust. 'It's just Alexi,' I added, for about the fiftieth time that day.

'You smell different to my mummy,' he murmured.

I let out a hoarse chuckle at the sleepy observation. 'I know,' I said as Belle directed me through the house towards the boy's bedroom.

'I like your smell,' he said, then rested his head on my shoulder, his fingers threading into the short hairs on my neck, and dropped back to sleep.

The simple statement had the rush of emotion surging through me so strongly, I had to lock my knees as Belle opened the door to his bedroom and turned on a night light beside his bed.

I stood holding my son, *our* son, for a few moments as she pulled back the duvet, my hands cradling his body, feeling his breath against my neck and inhaling his sweet scent. I knew in that moment I never wanted to let him go even as I forced myself to place him on his bed.

'Why don't you go into the living room and pour yourself a drink?' she whispered as she began to strip the sleeping child, her movements fast and efficient.

I nodded and walked out of the room, trying to control the emotion in my chest that was making it hard for me to breathe.

I walked through the living room and onto the balcony, and took a few steadying breaths of the sea air. But as I stared at the lights of Nice in the distance, just starting to illuminate the coastline, one devastating truth occurred to me. I would never again be able to dismiss the emotion this small boy stirred in me—because he was mine.

What surprised me more, though, was the realisation that I did not want to.

CHAPTER THIRTEEN

Belle

AFTER TUCKING CAI into bed, I made my way down-stairs to the house's large living area.

Where was Jessie? I needed her here as a buffer.

I had seen the rush of emotion on Alexi's face as he'd held Cai so carefully, so gently, as if he were the most precious thing in the world.

He had been wonderful with my son… I swallowed heavily…with *our* son all day. He'd answered all Cai's questions, talking to him in a way that acknowledged he was a child while also acknowledging he was an individual. A difficult balancing act few people in-stinctively knew how to do. But Alexi did.

Watching Alexi with Cai had brought back bitter-sweet yet beautiful memories of his close relation-ship with Remy.

Alexi, underneath the caution, the control, the commanding personality, had always been a sup-portive and kind brother, and it seemed he would be exactly the same as a father.

The joy of watching the two of them begin to form a bond—as they'd chatted about cars or had chased each other in a wild game of tag on the beach—had been intense at times, but it had also brought with it regret, confusion…and fear.

I needed to be careful. Alexi's relationship with his son did not change his relationship with me.

But as I walked into the living room and glimpsed Alexi standing alone on the balcony, his pensive expression lit by the lights of the city and the gold of the sunset, I felt the reaction I had struggled to ignore all day ripple over my skin.

The chemistry was still there and still unbearably intense—last night had not dimmed it in the slightest. That one searing look he had given me in the car had proved that beyond a doubt.

'Would you like a drink?' I asked.

Alexi turned and shook his head.

I trembled, blaming the breeze that drifted in from the balcony, even though the evening was warm.

I should go and join him, talk to him, thank him again for the wonderful day he had given Cai…and myself. But I knew I couldn't talk without babbling, and the balcony felt too intimate, my thoughts too volatile, to allow me to get that close to him. So I detoured to the sideboard, planning to pour myself a drink. And spotted a note in Jessie's handwriting propped on the dining table, addressed to me.

I picked it up and flicked it open.

Hey Cuz,
I hope you and Alexi and Cai had a fabulous
day together. I've decided to take a last-minute
trip to Paris and finally see the City of Lights,
like I've been promising myself for ever!
I'll make sure I'm back before you start
work—just text me if you need me in the mean-
time.
Alexi seems like a good guy—he's also su-
per-hot! I'm sure the last thing you need right
now is your old maid cousin cramping your
style.
You can thank me later.
Jess xx

I screwed up the note with shaking hands.
Oh, Jess, what have you done?
My cousin wasn't an old maid—she was younger
than me, having taken me in when she was still in
catering college. And she wouldn't have cramped my
style. If anything she would have been an important
safety valve. One I desperately needed as I stole another glance at Alexi's silhouette standing in the sunset looking proud, indomitable and… Yup, super-hot.

My cousin had deserted me in my hour of need. In
fact, she'd gone over to the dark side—encouraging
rather than curtailing the madness that had overtaken
my senses the night before. Unfortunately, the same
madness was coursing through my veins once more.

As I struggled to control the wave of excitement
and need, the weird mix of panic and validation at

Jessie's desertion—and attempted to make a sensible decision about what to do without our chaperone in residence—Alexi turned, almost as if he'd sensed my struggle and decided to intervene.

I could feel his gaze rake over me as it had in the car, igniting every inch of exposed skin.

'Stop hiding, Belle, and come here,' he said, his expression full of the same intensity I had seen on his face as he'd lifted Cai out of his car seat and held him close. But this time his expression wasn't stunned—it was raw and turbulent.

The need throbbed and ached at my core, but I couldn't seem to stop myself from crossing the room towards him.

When I reached him, he cradled my cheek, the rough calluses of his palm stroking the sensitive skin.

'Where is your cousin?' he asked.

So he'd noticed Jessie's absence too. He had to know how much more volatile the situation between us would become without her here.

'She…she left a note,' I babbled, the burning sensation becoming overwhelming as his head lowered to mine.

'What does it say?' he coaxed, before his warm lips settled on my neck, licking and nibbling the pulse point.

I gasped, sobbed, as he rubbed his mouth against my collar bone in an erotic rhythm that blurred my already dazed senses.

'She's…she decided to go to Paris for a while,' I

managed to choke out around the lump of need and desire throbbing in my throat.

His head lifted, his gaze fixing on mine. He framed my face in his hands, his fingers threading into my hair.

'Good,' he rasped, before covering my mouth with his.

The kiss was harsh, searing, demanding, leaving me breathless and limp when he reared back. He gripped me under my arms and lifted me against him.

'Wrap your legs around my waist,' he commanded. I did as he told me, unable to deny the need surging through me like a tsunami.

It still scared me, still shocked me, how quickly, how undeniable, the need was with him. How it seemed to daze all my senses and destroy all my objections. But as he marched through the living room and down the corridor, to the stairs leading to the bedrooms on the floor above, I could do nothing but cling to him and let the riot of sensations surge through me.

'Which door is yours?' he asked, his voice hoarse with need as we reached the first-floor balcony.

I signalled to my bedroom, my voice having deserted me, the need so strong I knew nothing on earth would stop me from feeling that thick length inside me again.

He shouldered open the door and kicked it shut, then placed me on my feet.

My breath shuddered out as he dragged my T-shirt over my head, unhooked my bra and pulled it off. He filled his hands with my breasts, the tender flesh aching as he caressed me, then leaned down to capture one swollen peak with his lips.

I cried out, the sound echoing round the ornate furnishings and into the night through the open terrace doors.

I heard the zip on my shorts releasing, the sound loud in the quiet room, almost as loud as our laboured breathing.

He dragged off my shorts, and I heard the rip of fabric as he tore away my panties.

'I can't wait. I need to be inside you,' he said. For the first time I heard the tremble of uncertainty, the note of desperation in his voice.

It was like a spur to my already overwrought senses. 'I need you too,' I whispered.

He clasped my hips in large hands then turned me, bending me over the bed. I could hear fumbling, several curse words in Italian as he stripped off his own clothing, then his wallet landed on the bed beside my head. The rip of foil told me he was sheathing himself.

His large hands returned to my hips to steady me. My legs quivered, my senses so attuned to his I could feel the staggered rasps of his breathing beating in my sex.

His fingers slid through the slick folds, testing my readiness. I bucked, sobbed, as his touch glided over my swollen clitoris, tightening the coil in my abdomen, the pleasure already beginning to ripple and pulse.

'*Grazie Dio,*' he murmured against my neck, his

perfect English deserting him, his tone as tortured as I felt.

He covered my aching breasts with his hands, caressing the nipples, making sensation arrow down to my already molten sex. Then he held me steady as the huge head of his erection notched at my entrance and slid deep in one relentless thrust. My slick folds adjusted to take the full measure of him, the muscles clamping down as the pleasure surged anew.

'No,' he demanded, withdrawing sharply. My breath shuddered out as the pleasure dimmed and the torture increased.

'Don't come, *bella*,' he rasped. 'Wait for me.'

'I can't,' I sobbed, the pleasure on a knife edge, so close and yet so far away as I yearned to feel him deep inside me again.

'Yes, you can,' he said, tweaking my nipples, making them throb and ache.

I tried to focus as he slowly thrust back in, filling me up to the hilt again. I struggled to hold back the inexorable wave, my whole body shuddering, shaking with the effort as he began to move—out and back, thrusting deeper and deeper—forcing me to take every hard, thick inch.

My mind reeled, my senses sparking along every nerve ending, throbbing in every pulse point, but I clung to that high ledge as his thrusts became harder, faster, slicing through more of my control.

Sweat slicked my skin, my sex pounding in time with the punishing, relentless thrusts, until all I could focus on was the heavy weight possessing me, overwhelming me. Then he shifted, nudging that spot deep inside only he knew was there. The merciless stroke ignited the inferno and I could cling on no more, flying over as the coil released in a rush, the blast of heat incinerating me as the pleasure exploded.

My sobs turned to keening cries as the waves engulfed me. I heard his shout as the orgasm shattering me powered through him, destroying everything in its path. He grew even larger, harder, as the devastation gripped us both.

He collapsed on top of me eventually, rolling so as not to crush me. His palms caressed my tender breasts as his arms tightened around me.

We lay like that for an eternity, cocooned together, the sweat drying on our skin, his heartbeat punching my back, the musky scent of sex filling the air, his breath harsh against the damp tendrils on my nape. My own heart pummelled my ribs so hard I was surprised it didn't burst out of my chest. The tears of emotion I had hoped to control stung my eyes.

The sob seemed to come from nowhere as he held me in the darkness. I dug my teeth into my bottom lip to hold it back, tasting blood. I mustn't fall apart. Mustn't make this mean more than it did. I didn't want him to know how weak I was, how needy.

His lips nuzzled my nape and his arms tightened, making the ache in my throat worse.

'Non piangere, bella,' he whispered.

Don't weep.

I blinked rapidly, glad he couldn't see my face

and the struggle to hold the overwhelming emotions at bay.

'I'm not crying,' I said, willing it to be true.

'Bene,' he murmured, then he gave me one last squeeze and let me go.

Lifting off the bed, he dragged the quilt up to cover my naked body.

I gathered the quilt around me to stave off the sudden chill as he headed for the *en suite* bathroom.

I fixated on the glorious sight of his naked buttocks, limned by moonlight, to stop the emotions overwhelming me.

And tried to tell myself the instinct to make love to Alexi wasn't an emotional one, it was purely physical. A basic, animalistic urge I had never been able to control.

He returned a few moments later but, instead of picking up his clothing and getting dressed, he climbed into the bed beside me. He wrapped an arm around my shoulders and tucked me against his side.

The tears threatened again, so I swallowed them down. What was the matter with me? Why was I falling apart at the smallest show of affection?

Just because I'd expected him to leave, just because he'd never held me like this before.

I shifted, peering up at him in the darkness. His gaze was fixed on the horizon but his expression was impossible to read. I wondered what he was thinking. Then tried not to. Why did it matter? Despite his relationship to Cai, he had made no promises to me. And I didn't need him to.

'It's probably better if you don't stay,' I murmured before I could get too comfortable having him with me. His gaze shifted to mine.

His thumb stroked my cheek. 'Why?'

I breathed. There were so many answers I could give him.

That I hadn't agreed to become his lover.

That as far as I was concerned this was just another one-off brought about by an emotionally and physically exhausting day.

But I knew he'd see through those excuses to the truth beneath—that I was terrified I'd become too dependent on his care and support.

I had surrendered again, as he had known I would. All I could do now was learn how to manage the hunger, and not entertain any unrealistic hopes, until the chemistry between us died. As it inevitably would for him, if not for me.

Alexi had never had a long-term relationship to my knowledge. Our chemistry probably wasn't anything out of the ordinary for him, the way it was for me. He'd had lots of sex with lots of women, according to the gossip columns and blogs I'd scoured over the last five years while pretending not to.

I had to make sure I didn't become dependent on the sex or, worse, the attention. Which meant not reading too much into a simple post-coital hug. So I kept my voice even when I replied.

'Cai usually runs in to wake me up at the crack of dawn every morning. It could get awkward if he finds you here tomorrow.'

He let out a gruff chuckle. 'So our son is an early riser,' he murmured, hooking a tendril of hair behind my ear. 'Why does that not surprise me?'

I smiled, even though my heart swelled against my ribs, making it hard for me to draw a breath. Why did he have to look so much more breathtaking when he talked about our son?

I knew it was dangerous to enjoy this moment too much while my sex was still humming from that titanic orgasm. But as his thumb stroked my cheek, his gaze both protective and possessive, I couldn't seem to stop myself from basking in his approval. Just a little bit.

He pressed a kiss to my forehead. 'Go to sleep, *bella notte*. I'll make sure I leave before he wakes up in the morning, but I want to hold you tonight.'

'Why?' I rasped, then wanted to snatch the question back. Did it sound as needy and hopeful to him as it did to me?

His lips spread in a sensual smile. 'Because you gave me a beautiful son, Belle, and it's way past time I thanked you for him.'

I blushed at the sincerity in his voice and the fierce gratitude in his eyes.

I tucked my head under his chin, hiding my face as I blinked rapidly to hold back the tears.

'It was my pleasure,' I murmured, toying with the dark curls of hair on his chest. 'Cai is the best thing to ever happen to me, so I should probably thank you too,' I added, my voice breaking.

He pressed his palm over my hand to stop my fidgeting, then tucked a knuckle under my chin. He lifted my face until I was staring into those pure blue eyes, filled with so much heat, I shivered.

'I will leave before the boy wakes this time, but I wish to spend more nights in your bed and I see no reason to keep it a secret from him. As you say, he is a bright child and adaptable and I will always be a part of his life. Plus, we have a rare chemistry, which we would be foolish not to indulge while it lasts.'

While it lasts...

My heart stumbled over the end of his statement— Alexi was already putting an end date on this affair, something I needed to do too. But still it made me feel unbearably sad.

'Do you not agree?' he asked gently in his usual confident, pragmatic tone.

He was asking me to sanction our affair, to welcome him into my bed and my life—for a limited time only—as well as my son's life. The fear clawed at my throat for a moment. Could I really do this— jump into a relationship with him, knowing it would not last? Knowing that, when he tired of me, I would be discarded and replaced like all the other women? Knowing I would have to spend the rest of my life as we brought up our son together, seeing him and no longer being able to touch him, to taste him, to feel him inside me as I could still feel the imprint of him now?

But as he waited patiently for my answer, his thumb stroking my upper arm while he held me, I could see the determination in his eyes, how much he wanted me to say yes, and the fear clawing at my throat loosened its grip a fraction, and then a fraction more. The raw ache of desire flooded in to replace it.

He was the only man I had ever loved, the only man I'd ever wanted, the only man to whom I'd ever made love. He was the father of my son and the brother of my best friend, whom I still missed.

I had lost Alexi once and survived, and I was so much stronger now than I had been then.

Perhaps there was still a chance for us. Who knew? But one thing I did know was that I wanted him in my bed, and I wanted the chance to become an intimate part of his life, to get to know the man I had never really known before. If for no other reason than he would always be a part of my life now, and Cai's, whether we were sleeping together or not.

So I threaded my fingers back into the hair on his chest and said, 'Yes, I want that too.'

His quick grin dazzled me, the low chuckle of relief, as if he had been unsure of my answer, a sop to my ego as he lowered his mouth to mine and kissed me.

He drew back first, the sensual smile spreading across his lips. *'Mille grazie, bella notte,'* he said, the rough, sexy tone scraping across my nerve-endings.

I settled into his embrace and waited for the flush of pleasure to subside as I listened to his heart thud steadily beneath my ear.

As long as I didn't make the mistake of becoming infatuated with this man again, everything would be absolutely fine, I assured myself as I drifted into a deep, blissful and exceptionally erotic sleep.

CHAPTER FOURTEEN

Alexi

'THE BOY IS your son, Alexi, is this not so?'

I turned to my friend, Dante Allegri, and frowned, annoyed by the perceptive question, even though I had expected as much as soon as I had arrived at the Allegris' annual summer barbeque at Villa Paradis with Belle and Cai.

'You are an observant man, Dante,' I murmured as the knot in my gut tightened.

To distract myself and him, I smiled at his toddler daughter Celeste, who was perched on his hip and was staring at me with wide tawny-green eyes.

The child reminded me so much of her mother, Edie Trouvé—or, rather, Edie Allegri, as she had become two summers ago at my friend's lavish wedding. The knot in my gut took a new twist, a twist that felt suspiciously like envy.

An envy I did not understand.

It was true, once upon a time I had wanted Dante's wife for myself. In fact, I had flirted mercilessly with her three years ago at the high stakes poker game in Dante's casino in Monaco when both Dante and I had met Edie for the first time. When she had rejected my attempts to seduce her at that game, having had eyes only for my friend, I had got over it quickly— so quickly, I had taken another woman home to my bed that night. A woman whose name—and face—I couldn't even remember three years later.

My gaze tracked to Belle, who stood beside Dante's wife on the Villa Paradis lawn. She had Cai's hand gripped firmly in hers as he showed another boy his age the toy car I had given him that morning.

I forced my gaze off Belle, and back to Edie, trying to understand the stab of envy. Dante's wife looked beautiful in an elegant blue dress, even more beautiful than she had looked the night I had first met her—and wanted her. Today she looked composed, graceful, happy, carrying the baby bump of her second pregnancy—which Dante had announced earlier—with all the poise of a woman who had somehow managed to have it all.

But I didn't want Edie any more. If I ever really had. She, like so many of the women I had dated, had been nothing more than a passing fancy. Unlike the woman who stood beside her. My gaze returned to Belle, and the heat surged as it always did when I looked at her.

After three weeks of sex whenever we could fit it in around our commitments as Cai's parents, why hadn't the hunger for her dimmed, at all?

I devoured the sight of her slender curves in the fitted designer dress, emblazoned with poppies to match her vibrant hair, the way I had when I had picked Cai and her up for the drive to Monaco an hour ago.

This was our last outing together before Belle started work and I would have to travel to England for the Primo Grande race—and I was already feeling agitated at the thought.

Unlike Edie's, Belle's stomach was flat. I remembered kissing it the night before when we had retired to her bedroom after tucking Cai into bed together. Remembered exploring the soft flesh around her belly button with my tongue, then drifting lower to capture the sweet taste of her arousal, which I had become addicted to. The heat rushed through me all over again as I recalled her broken sobs as she'd bucked and cried out against my hold.

I shook my head, trying to dismiss the memory. *Dio!* What was wrong with me? Why would this need not die? And why did it feel like so much more than just a physical hunger?

'If the child is your son, why have you not claimed him?' I registered Dante's question, tinged with incredulity and no small amount of judgement.

The accusatory look on my friend's face said it all. I bristled, but couldn't ignore the tinge of guilt. Dante was right. It had been several months now since I had discovered the boy was mine. And my relationship with Cai was going well.

I enjoyed spending time with him. I had taken him swimming and go-karting and tended to live at their villa when I was not forced to return to mine to catch up on work. The boy never stopped talking but I found his conversation fascinating. He still reminded me a great deal of Remy, but Cai was an individual too, his quirks and passions, his cheeky smile and sweet manner very much his own.

It was way past time I told him who I really was. I knew Belle would not object. In fact, I suspected she was becoming impatient for me to do so.

But, where once I had been keen to claim Cai as my son, now I hesitated. And I knew it had nothing to do with the child and everything to do with his mother.

'It's not as simple as that,' I said in answer to Dante's question. My friend frowned, not looking convinced. But then Dante had always been far too intuitive—it was one of the qualities that made him impossible to beat at the poker table.

'When did you discover he was yours?' he demanded, clearly affronted by my failure to claim my son.

'How do you know I did not always know and chose to ignore him?' I asked.

'Because I know you better than you think, Alexi,' he said, his eyes narrowing. 'You pretend to have no morals, but you are not a man to ignore his own flesh and blood.' He glanced to where Belle and his wife stood together, still deep in conversation. 'And the way you look at the boy's mother suggests she is much more to you than one of your casual conquests.'

The statement struck me square in the solar plexus because it was a truth I had been determined not to acknowledge until this moment. And it explained perfectly why I had been reluctant to claim the boy.

Fear.

Fear that claiming my son would only increase my need for his mother.

My hunger for Belle had not dimmed, and the more time we spent together, both as parents and lovers, the more it seemed to strengthen the bond—and only increase the chemistry that made me constantly want her.

And I hated that need.

After my brother's death—hell, even before it—with every woman but Belle I had been able to shut off my emotions. To keep them under lock and key.

I had no desire to do that with my son. He was a part of me, a part of Remy, and he could be better than both of us, with none of the scars we had borne from our own upbringing, if I made the effort. And with Belle's help I knew I could be a good father to him.

But with Belle? I didn't want to need her in any way other than the physical. It made me feel vulnerable and insecure, exposed and weak in a way I hadn't felt since I'd been a boy...and I had watched my mother climb into her lover's convertible and disappear into the night without a backward glance.

'You're right,' I murmured.

Why was I giving Belle this kind of power over me? Claiming the boy had no bearing on my relationship with her. We'd already established that before we'd embarked on this affair. I'd made her no promises, nor had she asked me for any.

The strange spurt of envy returned, still making no sense. I didn't want her to ask me for more than I was willing to give. Why the hell would I?

'I am?' Dante said, obviously surprised by my capitulation.

Ignoring him, I strode across the lawn towards Belle and my son. The boy let go of his mother's hand and ran into my arms. I hoisted him up and his small fingers gripped my neck.

'Mr Alexi, I showed Jean-Claude the Galanti X,' he said, shoving the model under my nose. 'He said it was cool.'

'Of course he did,' I said, catching Belle's eye. 'Belle, could I talk to you—and Cai—alone for a minute?'

Her face flushed and Edie grinned. 'I told you so,' Dante's wife murmured as a knowing glance passed between the two women.

I had no idea what had been said, but I suspected I had been the subject when Belle's face heated even more.

'Yes, of course,' she said.

'If you need some privacy,' Edie said, her grin spreading, 'there are some steps leading down to a private cove behind the Japanese pagoda. Dante and I always go there when we need some alone time…'

I nodded and gripped Belle's hand, giving her no time to change her mind. Cai was excited at the sight of the beach, and after I had carried him down the steps I put him down and took off his shoes so he could paddle in the water.

'Only get your toes wet, Cai,' I told him. 'It's dangerous to go in too deep without me, okay?'

He nodded. 'Yes, Mr Alexi,' he said as he sped off. I sighed.

'What is it, Alexi, is something wrong?' Belle asked, her concern clear even though she had been careful not to show it in front of Cai.

'There is nothing wrong. I simply wish to get your permission to tell Cai who I really am.' I smiled, trying to hide my own nerves. 'I'm tired of being called Mr Alexi.'

'Okay,' she said. 'I think he'd be thrilled,' she added. Although, she didn't look thrilled. 'But why now?' she asked.

Because I've been a coward. Because it's way past time. Because I'll have to let you go soon. And before I do I must take this next step.

But I couldn't say any of that without exposing myself. So I settled for telling her the one truth I could acknowledge.

'Because I'm tired of not being able to kiss you and touch you in front of him,' I murmured, and before she could evade me I dragged her into my arms, desperate to feel her surrender.

She gasped but her lips softened against mine as I covered her mouth. The kiss became hungry and seeking instantly, as it always did.

'Why are you kissing my mummy?'

I ripped my mouth away first to see Cai standing in front of us, having returned from the water's edge.

He tilted his head, more curious than accusatory.

Belle's face lit up like a Christmas tree and she crouched down to talk to him eye to eye. 'Cai, it's okay, you don't have to be afraid. Alexi and I are...'

'Shh, Belle, let me explain.' I touched her shoulder to halt the guilty tangle of words. 'Come here,' I said to Cai. The boy slung his arm around my shoulders as I knelt beside him in the sand, the way I had once seen him do with his mother. 'I kissed your mother because I like kissing her,' I said.

His nose wrinkled at that. 'Why?'

'Because she is special to me,' I said, the fear returning as I realised the truth of those words.

'Why?' the boy asked again.

There were so many answers I could give to that question, but there was only one I could allow myself to acknowledge. 'Because she is the mother of my son.'

The boy's brow furrowed, and although I felt choked at admitting the truth to my son for the first time I could see I'd been too cryptic for a four-year-old to understand.

'You are my son, Cai—and I am your father. I am sorry I haven't been in your life before now, but I would like to be in it for a very long time to come.'

'You're my daddy?' The boy's eyes widened as he caught on, and then his gaze shifted to Belle. She nodded, and then sniffed, and I realised she was struggling to keep her emotions at bay.

'Yes, I am,' I said as the boy's gaze shifted back to me.

'Can I call you Daddy?' he asked.

'Of course,' I said and he grinned.

'Can I tell Imran?' he asked. 'His daddy doesn't own racing cars,' he added, the proud, sweet smile making my heart expand in my chest. I had been accepted, and all I had had to do was ask.

'Yes, you can tell Imran. We will tell everyone together,' I said. I gathered him close and hugged his small body to mine, but as I drew back he put his hands on my shoulders, a serious expression on his face, and asked, 'Can you kiss my mummy more, so you can make me a baby brother, like Imran's mummy made him?'

I coughed, shocked not just by the innocent request but the surge of heat it brought with it—at the thought of making more children with Belle. The sudden urge to see her belly round with my child, the way Edie's was with Dante's, brought the surge of envy I hadn't understood earlier into sharp, too sharp, focus.

What I felt for Belle wasn't just sex. It had never been just sex. I knew that. But suddenly the amount I did feel for her—the visceral desire to make another child with her—terrified me even more.

My ties to my son, and before him to my brother, I understood. They were my flesh, my blood. I owed them my honour, my loyalty and what was left of my heart that I still had to give.

But binding myself to a woman—wanting to make my relationship with Belle any more permanent than it already was—that could not happen. I could not allow it to happen. Because the only woman who had ever had such a tie to me had broken it at her earliest convenience. And almost broken me at the same time.

The panic tightened around my ribs. I couldn't need Belle this much. I didn't want to need her this much.

'Cai, stop being so cheeky,' Belle said, looking flustered.

'Why is it cheeky? Imran said that's what happens when his mummy and daddy kiss too much.'

I choked out a strained laugh at the child's precocious explanation. But the claws digging into my chest were of fear. A fear I recognised from long ago, when my mother had deserted Remy and me after I had begged her to stay.

'It's cheeky because you shouldn't keep asking Alexi for things,' Belle said.

Cai leaned into me, his arms wrapping around my neck in a possessive gesture. 'But he's not Mr Alexi any more,' he said. 'He's my daddy.'

I chuckled, attempting to let the surge of love for this bright, cheeky child overwhelm the rush of panic as I gathered him close and stood up. 'Yes, but you should still always do what your mother tells you,' I murmured.

We made our way up the steep steps from the beach back to the barbeque and I announced my relationship to Cai to the party guests. The surge of pride I felt at finally announcing our relationship was tempered by deep unease. And a desperate loneliness that only made the panic more acute.

We could never be a real family. We would never

fulfil Cai's wish for a baby brother or sister. Because I could not expose myself again to the same devastating betrayal I had suffered as a child.

Which brought me to only one conclusion. I would have to cut this tie to my son's mother tonight, before it got the chance to cut me.

CHAPTER FIFTEEN

Belle

I GRINNED ACROSS the console at Alexi as he parked the Galanti GL8 in the garage under the house. Something wonderful, something immense, had happened today at the Allegris' summer barbeque. Something I hadn't expected but still felt so exciting, so new—unleashing all the feelings I had held in my heart for Alexi, not just for the last three weeks, but for the last five years.

When he'd announced to Cai that he was his father, with such tenderness, such humour and such understanding, it had felt as if the last bit of the wall between us was finally beginning to crumble.

But what had finally shattered it was the look he'd given me as he'd announced to everyone there that Cai was his son.

I hadn't really realised how desperate I had been for him to make this final move in the last few weeks—weeks of awesome sex and even more awesome family outings—until he had finally said the words out loud to all the people who mattered to him.

Edie Allegri, with whom I had bonded instantly the minute I had met her, had been the first to congratulate me. And something she had said to me earlier—just before Alexi had stalked across the lawn to ask to talk to Cai and me privately—had been ringing in my head ever since.

'Isn't it odd?' she had said with a knowing look in her eye that at the time had made me feel more than a little inadequate. Edie Allegri was a stunningly beautiful and an extremely confident woman. Not just confident in her career and her abilities as a mother but, from the way Dante looked at her, also one hundred percent confident in his love for her. 'I've always thought of Alexi as handsome, charming and amusing, but also careless and shallow. I never could figure out how he had become so successful in the Super League when he didn't seem to take anything seriously.'

'Alexi takes the business of racing very seriously,' I had said, jumping to his defence, but also confused by her description of him. I didn't recognise it at all. Not only was he a brilliant businessman, but I'd always found him to be the opposite of careless and shallow. Our relationship in the last few weeks had been so intense, but even as a younger man he had always been serious. I knew he had a reputation as a playboy, but it had never really occurred to me what that might mean.

Before I'd had a moment to process the thought,

Edie had smiled at me and added, 'He also takes *you* very seriously, much more seriously than any of the other women he has introduced us to. He certainly seems to have bonded with your son.'

I had murmured some platitude about him being a good man, sick that I was still having to lie publicly about his real relationship with Cai.

But as I sat opposite him in the car now—after everything else that had happened since my conversation with Edie—the hope that I might be different from all the other women in his life came back. But this time it didn't feel ludicrous or misplaced any more.

He had acknowledged Cai this afternoon, but by doing so it felt as if he had also acknowledged me. Intimacy had been growing between us these last few weeks—every time he touched me with such passion, every time he spoke to me with such respect, every time he strengthened his relationship with our son, while being sure to include me.

And the moment Cai had innocently mentioned getting us to 'make him' a baby brother I had seen the same flash of intense yearning in his eyes, when they had met mine, that was echoing in my heart.

Was it possible he wanted to make us a real family as much as I did?

I hadn't dared hope for that. I'd been trying in these last weeks not to expect too much from him. Not to let all the old fantasies devour me again. But we had turned an important corner tonight and I was tired of being a coward.

I reached across the console to rest a hand on his arm as he turned off the ignition.

'Thank you for today, it's been…' I laughed, so full of hope for the future I thought I might burst. 'Pretty special for me and Cai.'

'Good,' he said, sounding oddly perfunctory.

I dismissed the flicker of concern. Alexi was a serious, intense guy. He'd never done gushing, or light-hearted, or certainly not with me.

He glanced back at our son fast asleep in his car seat with the toy car Alexi had given him that morning still clutched in his fist.

'Let's get him to bed,' he said.

Need prickled over my skin and joy echoed in my heart as we exited the car together and Alexi lifted his newly acknowledged son out of his child seat.

We'd been through this ritual nearly every day for the last three weeks—putting Cai to bed together then retiring to my bedroom, where Alexi would invariably rip my clothes off in his urgency to feed the hunger which had been stoked to fever pitch as we'd avoided touching during the day.

Perhaps we wouldn't do that so much any more, not now that Alexi had kissed me in front of Cai and explained the situation to him. I wondered vaguely if I'd miss that urgency.

I grinned at the silly direction of my thoughts as we closed the door on Cai's bedroom after tucking him into bed and kissing him goodnight, the electric attraction buzzing in the air between us. Our hunger would always be volatile, exciting and full of heat—no amount of PDAs was going to defuse that.

But as I pressed myself against Alexi's body and flung my arms over his shoulders—planning to take the initiative tonight—he jerked back and caught my forearms.

'Don't, Belle,' he said, drawing my arms down to my sides. 'We can't, not tonight.'

'Why not?' I asked, shocked by the rigid expression on his face, especially as I could see the heat in his eyes and I had felt the beginnings of an impressive erection.

He gave my wrists a gentle squeeze, then let me go. He took a step back and raked his fingers through his hair. But he didn't meet my eyes when he spoke. 'I need to leave. I've got an early flight to London in the morning. And you're starting work at Galanti tomorrow.'

'Oh, I see.' Although I really didn't see. He had to leave early most mornings to avoid Cai finding us in bed together. My heart kicked into overdrive again at the joyful thought we wouldn't have to hide that from our son any more because it was totally normal for children to know that their parents shared a bed. I grinned at him, despite my disappointment. 'I'll take a rain-check, then,' I said, trying out the flirtatiousness I was still learning. 'And I appreciate you being so thoughtful about my new job. I'd hate my boss to think I was slacking on my first day after spending all night in bed with him.'

But as I leaned up on tiptoes to give him a teasing kiss, which I hoped would make him regret his decision, he pulled away again, his eyes strangely guarded.

'I don't think you understand, Belle,' he said, his expression cold now, as well as rigid. He was starting to scare me. Why did he seem so distant all of a sudden? 'There'll be no rain-check. This is the end of our affair.'

'What?' I gave my head a shake, sure I must have heard that wrong. Had he just said…?

'You're going to be working for me, Belle, and I don't screw around with my employees.' His gaze raked over my figure—the heat in it somehow insulting. 'However tempting.'

'But…'

But I'm not just an employee. I'm the mother of your son, and I love you.

The admission exploded in my heart. It was the first time I had ever been brave enough to truly acknowledge it, even to myself. But it wouldn't come out of my mouth, because right alongside it was the fear that had always stopped me from articulating it in the past. The fear that he would reject my love the way he had before. And that fear was real, raw and vivid now. As was the memory of the long-ago rejection I had struggled to recover from once before. I had thought it could never hurt as much again. I realised how wrong I had been as my heart shattered in my chest.

'But what?' he asked. 'I thought you understood we were simply scratching an itch here. You're not a child any more. You've slept with other men—you know how this works.'

But I haven't slept with any other men and I don't want to know how it works for you with other women. I thought I was different. I thought I was more.

The pleas died inside me, frozen out by the chill creeping through my body, the humiliation almost as excruciating as the pain. A pain I had to hide as best I could, or I would be reduced to nothing again, the way I had been once before. A nothingness I couldn't afford to inhabit again because I had a son.

We had a son.

I tried to cling on to that as I nodded and closed off the aching pain in the pit of my stomach.

The sting of the tears I was holding back felt like acid burning my eyeballs. I blinked rapidly and nodded again, forcing what I hoped was an approximation of a smile to my face.

Don't let him see you break. Pride is all you have now.

Thank God I had never told him the truth about my so-called other lovers or I would have been even more reduced now, even more vulnerable.

'Okay,' I said in a brittle voice which I could not let break. 'Well, let me know when you next want custody of Cai. We should probably arrange proper visitation rights.'

'I'll get Etienne on it,' he said, his gaze searing into my soul. But I forced the hurt down, desperate to keep it hidden just a little longer. 'I'll give you both a call when I get back from London to make arrangements.' He nudged a shoulder towards the stairs. 'I'll see myself out.'

'Okay,' I whispered again. But he had already walked past me.

It seemed to take no more than a second for his footsteps to pad down the hallway and for the front door to slam shut.

It took longer than an eternity, though, for me to control the painful sobs that consumed me once I had watched his brake lights disappear around the bend in the coast road from the balcony of the room we had once shared.

CHAPTER SIXTEEN

One month later

Alexi

CAI GIGGLED DELIGHTEDLY as we were both sprayed with champagne by Team Galanti's drivers—Rene Galoise and Ludovic Seveny—who had just taken the top two positions at the Italian Primo Grande Race. Cai bounced in my arms, adoring the attention—and the chance to join me next to the winners' podium after the race—as Rene and Ludovic high-fived him. I should be celebrating too, but I couldn't help searching the crowd for his mother.

Where the hell was she? It was her job to be here. I could have her fired if she didn't show.

I had insisted all my R&D staff attend the race today and the celebration event afterwards in Milan. But I had known, as soon as I'd had Pierre send out the emails a week ago, there was only one person I really wanted to see here.

Belle.

'Daddy, Daddy, can I go to the party tonight?' Cai placed his hands on my cheeks to turn my gaze back to him. 'Rene said I could.'

'I am afraid not,' I said. 'You will have to stay at the hotel tonight with Carly,' I added, naming the nanny I had employed for when I had care of him. Cai usually adored spending time with her in the evenings, on the rare occasions when I had to attend events without him, but even so his bottom lip quivered.

'But, Daddy, I want to,' he said.

I steeled myself against the adorable pout, which I had discovered in the last month my son was a master of applying, and the tantrum I had no doubt was coming. Cai had been at the track all day with me, eating junk food and getting everything he desired, because I was always tempted to spoil him when he was with me. But there was usually a price to pay for that.

Tonight, though, was an adults-only affair. An adult affair that his mother was supposed to be attending. His mother whom I had not seen for over a month. Not since the night I had walked away from her.

Ever since I had returned from London, she had endeavoured never to be at the villa in Nice when I came to pick up Cai or drop him off. And at work I had made a point of avoiding her.

I hadn't lied completely about not wanting to complicate our working relationship. But that was going to stop. Tonight.

Because I missed her—much more than I had

thought possible. Not just her passion, her hot, responsive body and the time we spent together with Cai—she certainly was much more skilled at dealing with that pout than I was—but also her smile, her wit, her tenderness, her intelligence and that captivating sparkle in her eyes whenever she'd been testing out her flirtation skills on me. I even missed her blushes, those vibrant flashes of red that made her freckles light up her face.

I wanted her back in my bed again. In my life. But I'd had to steal myself against approaching her at work. I didn't want to step over that line, compromise her, myself or the incredible job she was doing on the new prototype, according to my R&D manager, Ben Allison. But I had been forced to break even that embargo a week ago when I had composed that email.

I had ended our affair too soon. I wasn't over her yet, not completely. I'd allowed my fear to drive my actions, which was pathetic and beneath me. Why should we not continue our affair in private while co-parenting our son? How else was I going to get rid of this grinding sense of loss whenever I thought about her, which was far too often?

But despite that I did not want to make the first move. I had made a decision to get her to attend the race, assuming she would come to find her son—and me—as soon as she arrived. But I hadn't seen her at all.

Agitated and frustrated, I tapped out a text to Pierre on my phone.

Did Belle Simpson get on the Galanti jet with the rest of the R&D staff, this morning?

The reply popped up on my phone.

Yes, Alexi, she is here... Somewhere. I think I saw her chatting to Renzo Camaro and one of his technicians earlier.

I frowned. Why was she talking to Camaro? She didn't work for him any more, she worked for me.

I stifled my temper and shoved the phone in my back pocket. Didn't matter. The point was, even if she hadn't come to find Cai and me today, she would be at the event tonight. I had arranged for Carly to stay with our son until the morning, giving me ample time to seduce his mother.

Cai started to cry as I calmly and firmly explained to him again that he would not be going to the party.

He rubbed his eyes, so I hugged him a little closer. He was tired and cranky. I needed to get him back to the hotel and into bed.

But as I headed through the crowd towards the car park, still searching for a glimpse of Belle, a thought occurred to me.

Was Belle avoiding me deliberately?

Warmth and regret flooded through me. Why hadn't I seen the obvious before now? Of course she was avoiding me. I had rejected her. And her pride had forced her to hide the hurt I'd caused.

I promised myself that tonight I would correct that mistake. I would show Belle how much I respected her, and her work, and tell her I wanted her back.

I was the one who had ended our affair too soon. So I was the one who needed to make this first move.

The surge of passion and possessiveness was joined by the visceral need that had terrified me a month ago but didn't scare me so much any more.

I'd proved I could live without Belle for a month, but why live without her any longer if I didn't have to?

CHAPTER SEVENTEEN

Belle

'You look exquisite tonight, Belle.' Renzo's smile was full of appreciation and just a hint of more. If I wanted it.

A part of me wished I did.

Dressed in a tailored grey designer suit, Renzo looked impossibly handsome tonight—tall, dark and Italian. Even the scar on his cheek only added to his rugged masculine beauty. He had always been kind to me both as an employer and now as a friend. But unfortunately he didn't make my heartbeat accelerate whenever he was near me. And nothing about him made me yearn for his touch. His taste. His approval.

Even so, I forced what I hoped was a flirtatious smile to my lips. Tonight I was determined to try.

It had been a month since Alexi had walked away from me, and I had spent more than enough time grieving the loss. And beating myself up about how foolish I had been ever to believe we could have had more than a quick fling.

He had devastated me again. But this time I had let him by investing much more in that relationship than had ever been there. Alexi would be here tonight to celebrate another triumph for the Galanti team, no doubt with a new supermodel on his arm, and I wanted to be able to greet him without giving him even a hint of how destroyed I had been by his desertion.

I'd cried pitifully that night, but had picked myself up the next morning to be a mother. The first few days had been exceptionally tough as I started my new job—terrified that Alexi would appear, but thankfully he never had. And eventually the work, and Cai, had saved me from sinking further into the pit. I knew it would probably be a very long time before I would ever want another man the way I had wanted Alexi, but I had to stop hiding.

It wasn't good for Cai and it wasn't good for me either.

I refused to let Alexi have that power over me. He'd been callous and unkind, but he was still my boss, and I didn't want to jeopardise my career with Galanti over something that had always been doomed to failure.

Alexi wasn't capable of trusting women. In the back of my mind, I had always known that.

'Are you absolutely sure I can't tempt you away from Galanti?' Renzo carried on talking as he whisked a glass of champagne off a passing tray and handed it to me. 'I'm still annoyed he managed to tempt you away from me in the first place.'

I sipped the champagne.

'I'm afraid not, Renzo, but I'm happy to let you keep trying,' I teased, from the marble balcony where we'd positioned ourselves as my gaze darted once again to the entrance of the Grande Palazzo Hotel's elegant ballroom.

My heart thrummed in my chest.

Cai was staying in the hotel with Alexi and his entourage. I'd seen the two of them together earlier in the day at the track on the winners' podium from my seat in the stand. That I hadn't been able to get up the courage to approach them both afterwards, to congratulate Alexi on the team's win and check on my son, had made me realise I had to get over the last of my feelings for Alexi and close for ever that deep well of sadness—and unrequited yearning—that still overwhelmed me every time I thought of him.

It wasn't healthy, and it wasn't fair on our son. I'd been a coward once before and Cai had suffered. I wasn't going to do that again.

So stop looking for him like a lovelorn little girl. You're over him.

I forced my gaze back to Renzo and the fanciful spires of the Duomo di Milano, lit by the setting sun in the distance. And willed my fingers to relax their grip on the champagne flute as Renzo continued to flirt with me.

When Alexi finally showed I would be professional and impersonal. I would show him that I had survived, that I wasn't enthralled by him any longer and that he hadn't broken my heart. Because he really hadn't. All he'd done was bruise it a little. My heart was strong, because it had had to be. But as Renzo and I began to chat about the latest Galanti X model—with Renzo gently probing for information I had no intention of giving him—I could still feel the pulse of sadness that had never really gone away since Remy's death.

I took another gulp of champagne and dismissed it, as I had a million times before.

I was strong. I was a survivor. If Remy's death hadn't broken me, nothing ever could. Not even losing Alexi.

Alexi

As I entered the ballroom, I scanned the crowd, keeping a lid on my frustration as friends and acquaintances accosted me to offer their congratulations.

At last my gaze snagged on the open doors across the ballroom. And the longing that had been gripping my chest for weeks sunk deep into my abdomen, twisting my guts into tight knots of need… And fury.

The mother of my son, the woman who I had come here to get back, stood on the balcony with Camaro. A wispy dress of summer green hugged her slender curves, displaying her cleavage like an offering, her russet hair lit to gold by the sunset.

Abruptly cutting off the latest congratulations, I marched through the crowd, never taking my eyes off her.

How dared Camaro talk to her, flirt with her?

What secrets was he trying to prise out of her? The crowd parted to let me pass, probably sensing my foul mood, but then I saw her smile at him and a knife lanced into my gut.

Were they sleeping together?

I gritted my teeth as I stepped onto the terrace. My fury was only fuelled by the pain knifing into my stomach.

What the hell had I been thinking? Why had I let her go?

Renzo saw me first, his brows launching up his forehead, but then he smiled—the sensual, assured smile of a man who was in control—and the last thread on my own control snapped.

The wispy curls of Belle's up-do clung to her nape and my mouth dried to parchment, the urge to kiss her there, to make her sigh, sob and ache, and to drag her back into my arms—where she had always belonged—making my voice crack.

'Belle, we have to talk.'

She swung round, startled, and the champagne in her glass splashed over her fingers. The intense desire to lick it off turned the mix of pain, fury and bone-deep regret in my gut to something much more volatile.

'Alexi, is—is something wrong?' she stammered, her gaze shadowed. For a moment I thought I saw hurt there. But I couldn't be sure.

What was I doing here, behaving like a jealous lunatic?

What if I had been wrong about her needing me

as much as I needed her? What if she didn't care for me at all—any more than my mother had?

'Yes, Alexi,' Camaro said, the smile turning to a grin. 'What's the problem?' he asked, but I could see he knew exactly what the problem was, and he was deliberately making it worse.

Bastardo.

Another time, I would not have risen to the bait. But tonight my usual humour, my usual charm, my usual control, had deserted me.

He was standing too damn close to her.

I swore at him in Italian, gutter words I knew he would understand, because he came from the gutter, and that was where he belonged.

I grabbed the front of Camaro's suit and yanked him towards me. Belle gasped.

'Leave, now,' I growled in Italian. 'And never dare to touch her again.'

He only laughed, disengaging my hands, and brushed down the front of his suit. 'If you wanted her, perhaps you should have staked a claim,' he said to me, also in Italian, words he knew Belle would not understand.

But then he turned to her and bowed. 'Belle, I will leave you with your boss,' he said, lifting her hand and buzzing a kiss across her knuckles. I imagined knocking out his teeth. 'But remember, the offer still stands. *Ciao.*'

Saluting me, he strolled away.

'Come,' I said, grasping her hand, barely able to speak now round my fear. I forced my fury to the

fore—with Camaro, with myself—to try and stem
the terrible feeling of *déjà vu*.

Belle didn't care for me, because no one could.
Only Remy had. And I had lost him long ago—
without ever really deserving him. Any more than
I deserved Belle.

But Renzo was right. I should have staked a claim
to her. Bound her to me with sex. She was the mother
of my son. Surely that gave me a right to have her? A
right to want her by my side?

I marched to the opposite end of the balcony that
wrapped around the ballroom, heading for the entrance to the main lobby, clasping her wrist too
tightly, but unable to loosen my grip.

I had seen the flash of need in her eyes when she
had first laid eyes on me. She wasn't immune. There
was still desire there, a desire I could exploit. A desire
I *would* exploit. If sex was the only way I could make
her return to me, I would use it. And be grateful.

But as we reached the end of the terrace, she
tugged her hand out of my grasp.

'Alexi, stop, where are you taking me?'

I turned back to her and cradled her cheek, no
longer able to stem the urge to touch that soft skin.
'To my suite, where else?' I said as she shuddered,
the spark of desire in her wide eyes both gratifying
and torturous.

How had I ever let her go? *Why* had I? I couldn't
seem to make sense of any of my decisions any more.
My mind was a blur of long-ago fears and much more
current ones. Why had it never occurred to me until

this very moment that I could not live without this woman in my life? And it had nothing to do with the beautiful son she had given me. Or even the insane sexual chemistry we shared.

The pain twisted and sharpened in my gut as she jerked away from my touch and the spark of desire, the shadow of hurt in her eyes, died, replaced by something blank, shuttered and guarded.

Was she scared of me? The thought horrified me and humbled me.

Her whole body trembled, making me desperate to gather her in my arms and soothe her, promise her I would do anything to get her back. But the words got lodged in my throat, my own fear so huge now it consumed me. What if it wasn't fear I saw, but indifference? The same indifference I had seen flash in my mother's eyes when I had pleaded with her not to leave and she had simply laughed and left anyway.

But when Belle's gaze locked on mine and she spoke, she didn't sound scared or indifferent, she sounded brave…and indomitable. 'Whatever you have to say to me, we can talk here.'

'I don't want to talk, the time for talk is over,' I managed, frantic now, because I knew there was nothing I could say to make her stay. All I had now was our sexual connection. The cruel irony of that didn't escape me as I reached for her hand again, desperate to get her alone so I could touch her and tempt her, taste her and tease her, until she came apart in my arms as she had so often before…

Then I would never have to voice these terrible needs, never have to endure her rejection…

But she yanked her hand from my grasp.

'Don't touch me, Alexi, you have no right,' she said, her voice low and shaky but somehow unyielding.

It was too much.

The red mist that had descended when I had first spotted her smiling at Camaro returned. But this time I welcomed it to smother my fear.

'And Camaro does?' I snapped. 'Our bed is barely cold and you are already sleeping in his?'

CHAPTER EIGHTEEN

Belle

MY HAND WHIPPED UP of its own accord, Alexi's snarled words wounding me so deeply the anger surged from nowhere before I could stop it. But as his head reared back in an instinctive reaction to avoid the slap—a reaction I knew he had learned as a boy—my hand dropped back to my side.

I had never hit another human being in my life. And I had almost hit him. The horror of that was almost too much to bear. But as he watched me, his eyes guarded, the fortifying anger returned.

'You bastard,' I whispered. 'You were my first lover and you are my *only* lover, Alexi.'

His expression changed, going from anger to astonishment, tinged with stunned disbelief. The pain ground into my gut.

Why had I kept my innocence a secret? Why had I ever been ashamed of my lack of experience? Suddenly I didn't care how vulnerable it made me for him

to know he was the only man I had ever wanted...
Ever loved.

I had owned the mistakes I'd made—not telling
him of Cai's existence—but he had never owned
his. Because I'd never told him the truth. But, if I
never did, he would always have this power over me.
I would always be less than him. Why shouldn't I
own my feelings, own the love I had for him? If he
didn't want my love, he could reject me again, but I'd
be damned if I'd let him ride in and claim my body,
make this all about sex when for me if had always
been so much more.

'I've never slept with another man,' I said, grit-
ting the words out. 'Only you. I've never felt for any
other man what I feel for you. But that doesn't mean
you own me, not any more.'

I could still see the staggered incredulity in his
eyes and my heart shattered in my chest, just as it
had a month ago. Just as it had five years ago. For so
long I'd despised that foolish girl for her wayward
emotions but, as I stared back at him, I didn't despise
her any more. I had been right to feel what I did. The
mistake I had made was never to admit it.

Hiding my feelings to protect myself from hurt
had only allowed him to hide his too...

'I've just told you I love you, Alexi. That I've always loved you. Don't you have anything to say to
me?'

He blinked but then his face became the mask I'd
seen so many times before. The mask that kept him
safe. I knew that mask, because I'd worn it myself.

'How can you love me?' he finally said, sounding shocked now as well as incredulous.

'Really, that's all you have to say?' I said.

When he didn't speak, I huffed out a sad laugh that tasted bitter on my tongue. I hadn't expected a return declaration of undying love. But I had hoped for something, despite everything. One burning tear slipped over my lid and trickled down my cheek, his gaze tracking it as I brushed it away. 'Then I guess there's nothing more to talk about,' I murmured.

He didn't believe me. He didn't trust me. And now I knew he never would.

I turned to go, keeping my back straight and my legs as steady as I could. But as I took a step away I heard a choked cry.

'Wait! Stop…'

He grasped my wrist, but this time he didn't drag me back, only held on to me.

'Per favore, non andare,' he rasped. *'Per favore, non lasciarmi.'*

My Italian wasn't fluent, but I understood him.

Please don't go. Please don't leave me.

As I turned, to my shock he dropped to his knees and pressed his forehead against the back of my hand. It was an act of supplication, of penitence so real, so powerful, so naked that the hope I had thought was dead surged back to life, firing through my heart like a phoenix rising from the ashes.

His shoulders shuddered, and for one terrible moment I thought he might be crying. I wasn't looking at the man any more, I realised, I was looking at the boy, who had been abandoned all those years ago by a woman who should have loved him but hadn't loved him enough.

I sunk to my knees too, the marble cold against my shins as I gripped his face. His hard jaw flexed against my fingers as I lifted his head, the sheen of moisture in his eyes piercing my heart.

'It's okay, Alexi, I won't leave you,' I said. 'If you need me to stay.'

His breath shuddered out on a rasp of relief and he gathered me close, squeezing my ribs, my heart pummelling my chest so hard I was sure he could feel it.

'I do… I need you so much,' he whispered, his voice raw as he spread kisses over my cheeks, my lips, my neck, worshipping me with his mouth. 'I always have. Forgive me for never admitting it,' he said as he drew back, cradling my face to stare into my eyes, all the love in my heart reflected in the warm blue depths of his. He sighed, the shudder of breath reverberating through my body as he gathered me close, stroked my hair and held me to his heart as if he would never let me go.

'I was so scared to love you,' he said, his voice breaking. 'So scared that if I did I would lose you, the way I lost my mother. The way I lost Remy. The way I lost you when I turned you away. Can you ever forgive me?'

I pulled out of his embrace, the tears streaming down my cheeks now unbidden. But they were no longer tears of sadness, of heartache, they were tears of love. 'There is nothing to forgive,' I said, my voice thick with the happy tears.

A small drop escaped his own eye, but even as he scrubbed it away with his fist the emotion behind it pierced my heart.

It was a tear for us both, of sadness for all that we had suffered, for all that we had lost. And a tear of joy, for all that we had gained and would continue to gain. Together.

'There is *much* to forgive,' he said, but the wry smile that lifted his lips only intensified the joy. 'But I intend to spend the rest of my life making it up to you.'

Standing up, he offered me his hand. I took it and let him haul me off the cold stone and into his arms. The insistent heat rose to match the warm glow in my heart.

'If you will let me?' he asked, his hands settling on my waist as his gaze searched my face, still a little unsure, still so naked with need.

Love spread through me like wildfire—for this damaged, determined, indomitable man.

'Of course I will,' I said as I flung my arms over his broad shoulders and let his soft laugh wrap around my heart.

EPILOGUE

Three months later

Alexi

THE WINTER SUN warmed my face as I stood beside my brother's grave with Belle's hand gripped tightly in mine and our son perched on my hip. I had never had the courage to return to this place until today, scared the immense sadness—and the terrible guilt over Remy's death that had crippled me for so long—would return.

The deep, aching loss was still there, of course, as I knew it always would be, but I didn't feel hollow and empty any more. The hole in my heart was tempered by joy. Not just the remembered joy of being Remy's brother, but the new joy of being Cai's father and the all-consuming joy of becoming, as of an hour ago, Belle's husband.

I still missed my brother, I always would, and I knew Belle would too. Her slender body in the seductive white velvet wedding gown she had worn in the chapel as she'd pledged herself to me did nothing to stem the shudder of emotion running through her as her green eyes met mine. Her hand squeezed my fingers tight. Sweetly reassuring but also life-affirming.

'Who are we meeting here, Daddy?' Cai asked, his inquisitive blue eyes and that dimpled smile making my heart skip a beat. 'I can't see anyone.'

'We can't meet him, Cai,' I said, my voice rough as the sense of loss sharpened. I cleared my throat, determined finally to introduce my son to his uncle, the way I should have done months ago.

I knelt beside the grave, placing Cai gently on his feet to point out the grave stone. 'Because sadly Remy, my brother and your uncle, isn't here with us any more. But this is where he is buried. I thought we could come to his grave and say hello to him. Today is a very special day for us all because you and your mummy became Galantis.'

The surge of pride that had hit me earlier, when Belle had said, 'I do,' and Cai had leapt into my arms after our kiss, made my chest ache all over again. 'And Remy is a Galanti too.'

'Remy is my extra name,' Cai said, looking thoughtful.

'I know,' I replied. 'Your mummy gave you that name because she loved Remy too, just like I did.'

'Where did he go, Daddy?'

I heard Belle cough and sniff, and guessed the emotion was probably choking her the way it was choking me. But I sent her a smile and squeezed her fingers back.

'I've got this,' I mouthed at her.

'He went to Heaven,' I said to our son. 'But I know he would have loved to meet you.'

Cai wrapped his small arm around my neck and stared at the grave stone. 'Did he like racing cars, like I do?'

I let out a raw chuckle, the feel of his sturdy body beside mine—so trusting, so affectionate—making the emotion thicken my throat again. 'He liked racing cars the best of all, *just* like you do.'

'Will he come back? So I can show him my racing cars?' Cai asked.

I shook my head, not quite able to speak. 'No,' I managed at last. 'He can't come back. But he's here.' I pressed a hand to my heart. 'Always, just like you and Mummy are. Because I loved him very much, just the way I love you two.'

I scrubbed away the tear that slipped over my lid, but then I heard Belle stifle a sob.

Cai's head whipped around. 'Why are you crying, Mummy?' he asked. 'Are you sad?'

Belle shook her head, wiping her tears away with the heel of her hand as she sent us both a radiant smile. My heart expanded even more than it had an hour ago when she had walked down the aisle towards me in the stunning dress and Cai had skipped behind her, throwing petals around as if they were grenades.

'I'm sad and happy at the same time,' she said.

Cai giggled. 'That's silly, Mummy.'

'I know,' she said. Her eyes connected with mine over our son's head, the teary smile becoming tender. 'I'm sad that Remy isn't here, but happy that he'll always be with us in our hearts. And I know he would be so happy that we have each other…' She pressed a hand to her stomach, the way I'd noticed her do several times in the past week. 'And that we're going to have a new Galanti baby to join us in eight months' time.'

'*What…?*' I croaked, the joy and shock blindsiding me as Cai began to dance with excitement.

'You made me a baby brother with all your kissing!' Cai shouted. 'Just like Imran's mummy and daddy.'

Belle

'Yes, we did, Cai-baby, although we don't know yet if it's a brother or a sister,' I said to our son, who looked ecstatic as I grinned at Alexi's look of shock and awe.

I hadn't intended to tell Cai or him today. I'd only taken the test this morning to confirm my suspicions, and I was still reeling from the news myself.

The wedding preparations had been insane in the last few months after Alexi had insisted in Milan we marry as soon as possible. It must have happened during one of the many stolen moments we'd shared—in the shower, on the balcony, by the pool at night, and even one memorable moment at the test track in Nice after the rest of the staff had left for the evening—while frantically juggling our careers, family commitments and the wedding preparations.

We must have jumped the gun before the contraception I had started taking had become fully safe. We hadn't planned this, hadn't spoken about having another child, *yet*. But we *had* spoken about having another child eventually. Alexi was such a brilliant father, and we had both agreed we didn't want Cai to be an only child.

But hearing Alexi speak about Remy, standing over his grave, had just made it seem like the right moment to share the news. Why was I keeping it a secret? I'd married the man of my dreams today, and while I'd said my vows to my husband I'd felt Remy's presence by my side and had heard his voice in my head, laughing and saying, *It's about damn time you finally kept your promise to me,* bellisima.

'If I have a sister, can she play racing cars with me?' Cai asked, swivelling his head between the two of us.

'Of course she can,' Alexi said as he rose to his feet—still looking a little shell-shocked. But then he leaned close, gripping my cheeks with his usual confidence while sandwiching our son between us.

The broad smile that spread across Alexi's impossibly handsome features made my chest feel tight as Cai wriggled furiously and started to giggle.

'Galanti girls like racing cars too,' Alexi said to our son as he wriggled free. 'And I've got the bestest Galanti girl of all,' Alexi whispered against my mouth, before wrapping his arms around me and lifting me off my feet.

He swung me around, to Cai's delight—and a spontaneous laugh burst out of my mouth to match the joy I could no longer contain bursting in my heart.

* * * * *

WE HOPE YOU ENJOYED
THIS BOOK FROM
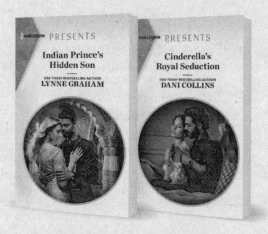
⟨H⟩ HARLEQUIN
PRESENTS

Escape to exotic locations where passion knows no bounds.

Welcome to the glamorous lives of royals and billionaires, where passion knows no bounds. Be swept into a world of luxury, wealth and exotic locations.

8 NEW BOOKS AVAILABLE EVERY MONTH!

#3813 A HIDDEN HEIR TO REDEEM HIM
Feuding Billionaire Brothers
by Dani Collins

Kiara could never regret the consequence of her one delicious night with Val—despite his coldheartedness. Yet behind Val's reputation is another man—revealed only in their passionate moments alone. Could she give *that* man a second chance?

#3814 CROWNING HIS UNLIKELY PRINCESS
by Michelle Conder

Cassidy's boss, Logan, is about to become king! She's busy trying to organize his royal diary—*and* handle the desire he's suddenly awakened! But when Logan reveals he craves her, too, Cassidy must decide: Could she *really* be his princess?

#3815 CONTRACTED TO HER GREEK ENEMY
by Annie West

Stephanie would love to throw tycoon Damen's outrageous proposal back in his face, but the truth is she must save her penniless family. Their contract says they can't kiss again...but Steph might soon regret that clause!

#3816 THE SPANIARD'S WEDDING REVENGE
by Jackie Ashenden

Securing Leonie's hand in marriage would allow Cristiano to take the one thing his enemy cares about. His first step? Convincing his newest—most *defiant*—employee to meet him at the altar!

YOU CAN FIND MORE INFORMATION ON UPCOMING HARLEQUIN TITLES, FREE EXCERPTS AND MORE AT HARLEQUIN.COM.

HPCNMRB0420

"No." He held on to her wrist as though he could tell she was
about to run from the room. "Stop."

Her eyes lifted to his and she jerked on her wrist so she could
lift her fingers to her eyes and brush away her tears. Panic was
filling her, panic and disbelief at the mess she found herself in.

"How is this upsetting to you?" he asked more gently,
pressing his hands to her shoulders, stroking his thumbs over her
collarbone. "We agreed at the hotel that we could only have two
nights together, and you were fine with that. I'm offering you three
months on exactly those same terms, and you're acting as though
I've asked you to parade naked through the streets of Shajarah."

"You're ashamed of me," she said simply. "In New York we
were two people who wanted to be together. What you're proposing
turns me into your possession."

He stared at her, his eyes narrowed. "The money I will give you
is beside the point."

More tears sparkled on her lashes. "Not to me it's not."

"Then don't take the money," he said urgently. "Come to the
RKH and be my lover because you want to be with me."

"I can't." Tears fell freely down her face now. "I need that
money. I need it."

A muscle jerked in his jaw. "So have both."

"No, you don't understand."

She was a live wire of panic but she had to tell him, so that he understood why his offer was so revolting to her. She pulled away from him, pacing toward the windows, looking out on this city she loved. The trees at Bryant Park whistled in the fall breeze and she watched them for a moment, remembering the first time she'd seen them. She'd been a little girl, five, maybe six, and her dad had been performing at the restaurant on the fringes of the park. She'd worn her very best dress and, despite the heat, tights that were so uncomfortable she could vividly remember that feeling now. But the park had been beautiful and her dad's music had, as always, filled her heart with pleasure and joy.

Sariq was behind her now; she felt him, but didn't turn to look at him.

"I'm glad you were so honest with me today. It makes it easier for me, in a way, because I know exactly how you feel, how you see me and what you want from me." Her voice was hollow, completely devoid of emotion when she had a thousand feelings throbbing inside her.

He said nothing. He didn't try to deny it. Good. Just as she'd said, it was easier when things were black-and-white.

"I don't want money so I can attend Juilliard, Your Highness." It pleased her to use his title, to use that as a point of difference, to put a line between them that neither of them could cross.

Silence. Heavy, loaded with questions. And finally, "Then what do you need such a sum for?"

She bit down on her lip, her tummy squeezing tight. "I'm pregnant. And you're the father."

Don't miss
The Secret Kept from the King,
available May 2020 wherever
Harlequin Presents books and ebooks are sold.

Harlequin.com